SWITCHED
by
Derrick J. Truesdale

To Jay and G
Good friends are hard to find, thank you!

Respect yourself and others will respect you.

— Confucius

ONE

Spring 2001

TERRY HARPERS' APARTMENT didn't look much different than the apartments of most single twenty-three-year-old men.

The one-bedroom apartment was modest in size and was located in one of the newer apartment complexes in Northeast Philadelphia.

Everything in the apartment was working. Everything in the apartment was new, so it should work.

In the living room, the space felt orderly in a way that felt intentional, not sterile. A beige microfiber sofa bed sat squarely against the wall closest to the front door, cushions firm and even all the way across, no sag in the cushions.

A wooden coffee table-dark brown, held exactly four things: a remote control, a coaster, a notebook with some algebra II questions unanswered and there was one pencil next to the notebook.

Perpendicularly adjacent to the Sofa bed and table was the front door to the apartment and a tube television, twenty-seven inches, maybe a Sony, rested on a dark brown compact stand. Beneath it: a neatly stacked row of CDs in cases. You might spot Nas, OutKast, Jay-Z, maybe some New Edition, DÁngelo, Maxwell, or Boys II Men, but nothing scattered, everything sitting up neatly.

The wall-to-wall carpet was vacuumed in visible lines, one pair of black on white Jordans sat comfortably by the front door.

The windows all had cream colored mini-blinds with black curtains all of which sported a black valence moving neatly across the top.

The kitchen was medium sized and designed as an open concept having a breakfast bar separating it from the living room instead of a wall and it was also clean to the point of being quietly impressive. There were off white appliances, no magnets on the fridge. Inside the cabinets, dishes were stacked by size, and all of the glassware was spotless.

Also in the kitchen, there was a drying rack which had one plate, one fork, and one glass, all cleaned after last night's dinner.

Also on the counter, a coffeemaker, a knife block, and an empty fruit bowl.

From the kitchen, passing the breakfast bar as you cut through the living room, there sat the bathroom.

The bathroom smelled faintly of soap and aftershave. The beige and black color coordinated towels inside hung neatly over the towel racks. The mirror was immaculately clean. There were no personal items like toothbrushes or razors sitting out, they were all kept in the medicine cabinet.

Across from the bathroom was the bedroom, calm, wearing neutral tones of black and gray. No loud patterns. The black lacquer dresser held folded clothes, socks, tee shirts, and under wear.

Hanging in the closet were pressed shirts, jackets evenly spaced, and creased pants.

Next to the bed, on the nightstand: a digital clock radio with the bright red numbers zero six twenty-nine, a lamp which was off, and a man's wallet carefully placed.

The radio blared Aretha Franklin's hit song '*Respect*' as soon as the digital alarm clock flipped to six thirty a.m.

♪What you want...ooh♪
♪baby I got it...ooh♪
♪what you need...ooh♪
♪you know I got it...ooh♪

Sleepily, Terry Harper looked at the time as he threw the blanket from overhead and slowly inched his way from off the bed.

Terry walked groggily over to the bathroom, lifted the lid to the toilet, and relieved himself of what felt like twenty gallons of fluids he had consumed the night before.

He then flushed the toilet and washed his hands.

♪all I'm askin...ooh♪
♪for...is a little repect♪
♪just a little bit...hey baby♪
♪just a little bit... ♪
♪R-E-S-P-E-C-T... ♪

As the song continued, Terry looked at himself in the mirror and smiled. He loved himself. He was an attractive young man, light brown skin tone, well defined chiseled torso and even well tapered haircut with two-to-three-inch locks at the top.

His face was clean-shaven and his teeth pearly white

Wearing only a towel, Terry started dancing while brushing his teeth in the bathroom mirror. After he rinsed his mouth out he joined the song. "I ain't gonna do you wrong...SYKE!"

As the music continued playing, Terry stood into the mirror, staring at his bare chest. He then started posing sideways and smiled at himself in the mirror.

"Yeah, I'm the shit!" he declared speaking only to himself.

***

The gym was already awake.

It always was at this hour, early enough that no one talked much, late enough that the serious people had already staked their machines. Terry liked it that way. No lines. No noise. Just motion.

He stepped onto the treadmill near the windows, set the speed without looking, and started running.

The belt hummed beneath his feet. His breathing settled into a familiar rhythm. Music filled his ears, something fast and aggressive, the kind that shut everything else out.

He glanced sideways and caught a guy on the next treadmill looking over.

Terry lifted his chin in a quick nod.

The guy nodded back.

That was it. There were no long and drawn-out conversations, no words of any kind. There was no reason for any.

Terry focused forward again, letting his mind drift as his body did the work.

Running had always been easy, automatic. Something he could disappear into.

A woman stepped onto a treadmill a few spaces down.

Terry noticed without thinking about it. Long ponytail. Bright top. Good form.

He watched her for a second too long.

Not enough to be creepy, at least not in his own mind, but enough that he caught himself and smirked, shaking his head as if to say *get it together*.

He sped up slightly.

Another woman crossed the floor toward the free weights. Terry's eyes followed, more out of habit than intent. He didn't feel guilty about it. This was normal man behavior. This was just... noticing and admiring.

Someone laughed near the benches in the midst of conversation with someone else, one coming the other going.

Terry wiped sweat from his brow forty-five minutes into his run with the back of his wrist and checked his time. *Almost done.*

He finished his run, slowed the treadmill, and stepped off, legs loose and warm. He grabbed his towel, passed the same guy from earlier, and got another nod in return.

Routine.

He moved through the rest of his workout efficiently, weights, stretching, a quick glance in the mirror to check his form. He caught his reflection and gave himself a brief, satisfied look.

Not bad.

By the time he headed for the locker room, he felt good, clear, loose, grounded. Whatever the day would throw at him, he'd already done something for himself and so was ready for it.

He didn't think twice about the looks he gave or the space he took up.

He didn't have to.

***

After he got back to his apartment, Terry immediately started tearing his clothes off and headed into the bathroom. He then turned the shower on and reached in, testing the temperature of the water.

While he waited for the water to get hot, he moved over to the toilet and peed.

After another minute, he rechecked the water and then got into the shower.

***

After getting out of the shower, Terry then spun around while listening to James Brown's *'I got the Feeling'* and danced over to his closet in order to pick out an outfit.

"Baby, baby, baby...baby, baby, baby...baby, baby, baby...baby baby...I got the feelin'"

He glossed through the closet while shimmying until he found a selection of clothing appealing to him and laid it across the bed. He then turned back around to face the mirror on his dresser but opened a drawer. "Lemme see, boxers or briefs?"

He carefully moved stuff aside in the drawers as a look of realization grew across his face.

He smiled.

"Boxer briefs!"

***

In the kitchen, now fully dressed, Terry was drinking a cup of coffee as he attempted to finish a couple of math problems in his notebook.

"Negative b...plus or minus the square root of four a - c squared...over two times a...no that's not..."

The ringing of the doorbell interrupted Terry and he gladly dropped the pencil down on his notebook and got up from the table.

"Yeah, I'll finish that later," he said out loud and to himself.

Terry then walked over to the front door and opened it.

As he opened the door he saw three of his friends; Jason, Guang Yu, and Greg .

Jason favored Terry a bit in looks, similar in skin tone and build, but Jason' hair was cut in a conservative low tapered style. That was pretty much where their similarities ended.

Jason was practical in his approach to everything unlike Terry who believed in his ability to conquer anything because of his masculinity. Especially women.

Guang Yu, immigrated from Canton China when he was ten years of age and Terry was the first friend he made. He later met Terrys' best friend Jason and the trio have been friends ever since. Physically fit and attractive, meeting women was never a problem for Guang, but like Jason, his focus was on academics.

The trio met Greg later in life, by the time they reached high school, he was a little smaller but just as fit as the others, but he often schemed to get things the easy way.

The other three guys often showed him that there were better ways to become popular, or get girls, or make money and since he enrolled in college right after high school along with his friends, his life was going in the right direction.

"Wuz up my nigga?" Guang Yu asked with a wild smile on his face.

Jason smacked Guang Yu on the back of the head as they both walked in. "Didn't I tell you to stop saying that? It's derogatory!"

Guang Yu flagged him. "That would only apply if I were white."

"Well you ain't black either," started Greg.

"Nix that," started Guang Yu as he strolled past Greg. "I'm more black than you!"

Annoyed, Greg flagged Guang

"He got you there," started Terry, "but in any case, it's derogatory, so let's chill on that."

"So what up?" asked Greg. "The jawn you ditched us at the party for the other night?"

"Don't even go there... Jay, you and G would've done the same thing, right?"

"Well I wouldn't had left y'all like that," started Greg.

"You wouldn't had left us at all," replied Jason as Greg flagged him.

Terry slapped hands with Jason and Guang. "What do you think happened?"

Greg smiled with excitement. "Yo...you finally hit that jawn from your chem class last semester?"

"I not only hit that jawn," bragged Terry, "but I pulverized that mother fucker."

Greg chuckled wildly. "Damn you a lucky nigga."

Jason hit Greg and Greg then turned around and threw his hands up defensively.

"Yo, don't be hittin' me," he said.

"Stop...using...the 'N' word," said Jay.

"What can I say?" asked Terry as he continued. "I got skills that kill in chemistry!"

Jason, who had walked into the kitchen, then looked in Terry's open notebook. "Your skills not gonna mean shit if you don't know how to do a simple quadratic equation on your exam Friday."

Terry strolled into the kitchen followed by Greg. "Yeah, I'll get it just gotta practice more, but Jay...you mind hookin' that up for me just one last time?"

Jason picked up the pencil and started working through the problem in the notebook.

Greg turned from Jason and faced Terry again. "So tell me dawg...how was she?"

Terry smiled at his own wonder. "Man she was so good, I thought I was havin' a seizure."

Greg laughed with excitement as Guang just shook his head in the negative.

"Maybe you should keep some diazepam rectal gel by your bed just in case you feel that way in the future," joked Guang.

"Rectal gel?" asked Terry. "This rectum here is an exit only!"

"In other words Greg," started Guang, "stop believing his bull shit."

Jay shook his head in the negative without looking up from the table.

"Anyway," started Terry as he looked over at Jason and then back at Greg. "After we got done, she kept goin' on and on about how she could see us getting old together and having children."

"After one hit?" asked Greg.

Terry nodded. "I told her it was too soon for all that talk and that I wasn't hardly ready for it."

"Why not?" asked Jay without looking up from the book. "It wasn't too soon for you to sleep with her."

Terry grew annoyed. "You need to loosen up, go get yourself a little more of the twizat."

"I think he needs more than a little," said Greg.

Jason looked up at the pair as he put the pencil back down on the notebook.

"I have no problem with getting what I want when I want it, I just have a little more respect for my sisters and myself then the two of you combined."

"He's right yo," started Guang Yu, "it's all fun and games but if you mess wit the wrong person...I'm just saying, you don't want those kinds of problems."

"Yeah whatever!" flagged Terry. "When y'all get body counts like mine, then y'all can give me advice."

"C'mon dawgs," started Greg as he looked between Jason and Guang, "we're your rowdies, you can tell us if you two are gay, we'd still love yall."

Terry laughed. "Not as much as Bernie would."

"I give up," said Jason with frustration. "Both of you will learn that sex is ninety percent emotional and ten percent physical."

Terry sighed. "Yeah whatever, all I want is that ten percent... look yawl ready to roll or what?" he asked changing the subject.

He then grabbed his coat, as they all started heading for the door. "Where are we picking Bernie up from?"

They started leaving through the door.

"Broad and Hunting Park," answered Jason as he closed the door behind him.

***

At Broad and Hunting Park, Jason's Dodge Durango pulled into the McDonalds' parking lot and parked.

"Where is he?" asked Terry.

Terry, Jay, and Greg were all looking around in different directions.

Greg then pointed. "There he is!"

They all turned in the direction of where Greg was pointing at for Bernard.

Bernard was the tallest out of the group. He stood at six foot three inches tall and was also physically fit. He was chocolate complexioned and wore a light full beard on his face.

Bernard knew Terry and Jason since middle school and though he was friends with all of them Greg never liked him that much.

Bernard looked around until he heard the car horn honk twice, he then pointed in their direction and smiled as he mouthed the word, *fellas*. He then quickly gave the man who was with him a kiss and started his way across the street.

Terry and Greg both looked away disgusted. "Aw damn!" they said simultaneously.

"Did he do that in front of us on purpose?" asked Greg. "He just gave that brotha a kiss."

Jason looked at Greg as if he were from another planet. "What'd you expect? Lamar is his man!"

Soon one of the doors of the Durango opened and Bernard got in. "Hey fellas, how yawl doin' this mornin'?"

"Hey Bernie!" replied all four, Greg with an attitude.

Bernard pulled his gloves off his hands. "Guess what Terry? You weren't the only one who got sum the other night...whew!"

Greg sucked his teeth. "Aw shit! Here he go!"

"I had me a ride on the tilt a wheel," continued Bernard. "I tell you there's nothin more satisfying than feeling a nice hard..."

"BERNIE!" yelled Greg, "we really do not need to hear this."

Bernard sighed. "Suit yourself, I thought you liked to hear sex stories." Bernard loved making Greg feel uncomfortable.

"I like to hear stories about man and woman," started Greg, "maybe woman and woman, but definitely not man and man."

"Besides Bernie," started Guang as he turned from the window, "You're already in a relationship so your stories don't count."

Bernard shrugged his shoulders and nodded.

"And they're man on man," Greg repeated.

Bernard tapped Jason on the shoulder as he was still driving.

"You're right," he started," he is definitely trying to avoid his homosexual nature."

Terry, Guang, and Jay all laughed as Greg looked at all of them with an angry expression on his face.

"Fuck all yall!" Greg finally said angrily.

***

Later in the day, inside the Community College of Philadelphia, Terry and his three of his friends, Bernie, Jay, and Greg were sitting in the cafeteria adjacent to the West Building.

Jason ran over and grabbed a tray, paid and returned to the table.

After Jason returned to the table with his lunch, Terry punched him in the arm.

"By the way punk," he started, "you know what you did was wrong."

"What'd I do?" asked Jason with a plaintive facial expression.

"Giving me the wrong answers on that take home test."

"Ooh!" sighed Greg as he turned his head and looked out the window.

"Oh that!" laughed Jason. "I had to teach you a little lesson somehow. At, least the mistakes were simple enough for you to correct."

"Well, you should have taught me that lesson at another time," started Terry. "Had me lookin' like an ass in class, putting the wrong answer up on the board."

Everyone started laughing as Anna Homestead walked over towards them apparently unnoticed.

"Then next time you'll do your own homework," said Jason as he looked up at the young woman who approached the table.

Anna Homestead was twenty-four, brown-skinned, and built with the kind of athletic balance that came from use rather than effort. Her body didn't announce itself; it *held* itself, shoulders naturally squared, spine straight, movement economical and sure. There was nothing exaggerated about her figure, only the quiet confidence of strength which had been earned and lived in.

Her complexion was warm and even, catching light easily, the sort of skin which seemed to glow softly rather than shine. When she moved, there was a subtle tension beneath the surface, muscle ready, responsive, giving the impression that she was always aware of the space she occupied and how to move through it.

Anna's face carried an understated attractiveness. Strong cheekbones framed expressive eyes that missed very little. Their focus often intent, thoughtful, as if she were always reading more than what was being offered.

Her mouth, full and naturally set, tended toward seriousness, but when she smiled it arrived without warning and changed the tone of her entire expression, quick, genuine, disarming.

She wore her hair in a way that made sense for her life rather than fashion, neat, controlled, practical, further reinforcing the sense that Anna valued capability over display. Even at rest, she looked prepared, as though stillness for her was simply another form of readiness.

"Hey Terry," she started as the other guys with him accommodated space to her so she could talk. "I thought you were gonna pick me up this morning."

Terry developed a phony confused look on his face. "Why would you think something like that?"

"Well usually when I'm told I'll be there by eight a.m. on Monday to pick you up, I usually believe that I will get picked up."

Terry flagged Anna. "I didn't drive, my fault!"

Anna grew annoyed by Terry's obvious disregard for her. "Look, all I'm saying is... you could've at least called and told me you weren't going to make it, I would have found another way to school."

Greg snickered and Jason tapped him on the arm hard, signaling him to stop.

Anna exasperated and looked at the guys at the table.

"I don't believe yawl, don't yawl know how hard it is out here for a sistah without her so called brothers screwing her around."

"Trust me child, I know," replied Bernard.

Anna shook her head in annoyed frustration.

"So Terry... all of ...Mister nice guy ... phony acting for the last three months was just so you can get a shot of pussy? I hope you're satisfied."

Terry sat his drink on the table.

"I was, thank you," he said ignorantly.

Jason dropped his head in disappointment at his friend. He then signaled for the rest of the group to follow him out of the booth.

"Ter, we'll meet you back here in about two, I gotta get to my next Jawn!" said Jay.

They all got up and left.

Anna got teary eyed and just stood there.

"You know, if I'd thought you were like this, I would've never wasted my time."

Terry looked away as if disinterested in what she had to say.

"Look Anna," Terry started, "you really wanna go on and on because I didn't give you a ri..."

"I'm pregnant Terry," she interrupted as he quickly looked away. "Do you even care?"

"Look I wore protection, so I don't know what you expect me to tell you."

Anna started tearing. "I don't believe in abortions, so..."

"Well that's your choice," said Terry. "Don't expect me to to..."

"Fine," she interrupted, "don't call me, and I won't bother you; my baby and I will be fine without you!" Anna started to walk away and then stopped.

"You know," she started, "maybe you need to feel what it's like to be on the other side of the fence, maybe you won't shit in the neighbors' yard." She then stormed off.

Terry seemed to be slightly bothered by her comment, but not by much.

"I would prevail no matter what side of the fence I was on, 'cause I can handle shit," he said out loud and to himself as he got up from the table and headed out the cafeteria.

In the booth sitting behind him was a young woman named Sorrie Cerhess, who overheard the whole interaction between Terry and Anna.

Sorrie had a negative interaction with Terry herself in the past and just chalked it up to 'lesson learned,' in her growth as a young woman, but she had never realized just how much of an asshole he really was.

Maybe, she thought, *him being on the other side of the fence isn't such a bad idea.*

Young Sorrie had been coming into her own as a Practioner of mysticism, a gift she earned from her Haitian father. She then decided she would further practice her skills on this misogynistic, narcissist who regularly objectified women.

***

The clouds started brewing as a storm started announcing its arrival in the Mount Airy and Cheltenham neighborhoods.

No storms were forecasted for the area, but this was noted to be the after effect of someone tampering with dark magic.

The few clouds lingering soon started to swim swiftly through the darkened sky as lightening flashed once just before her brother thunder.

KRACKOW!

Then again.

KRACKOW!

And finally a third time.

KRACKOW, the last thunder strike seeming louder than the first two thunder strikes.

Inside of her bedroom, Sorrie had a small picture of Terry Harper she cut out from her high school year book and she placed it next to a white candle.

She then folded her arms and looked upward. "Spirits of the Trinity hear my cry, I wish not to bring harm to this fragile guy, but because of the hurt he has caused in the past, I wish to teach him a lesson at last."

Sorrie lit the candle and then looked up to the sky as a light gust of wind blew her hair back a little.

She smiled. "Aequilibrium eius frange, orbem muta, et puer olim factus, in puellam adolescat."

KRACKOW!

KRACKOW!

KRACKOW!

The lights flicked off and then on with each thunderous bang and then suddenly, Sorrie could see the sky clearing up.

The wind soon stopped blowing so hard.

Quiet and peace returned to the neighborhood as if nothing had ever happened.

***

Terry quickly sat up in bed in a cold sweat.

He then looked around nervously and immediately relaxed and smiled as he admired his latest conquest who was still laying beside him sleeping soundly.

She was twenty-two, brown-skinned, and Afro-centric in a way that felt rooted rather than styled, beauty that came from lineage, not effort. She slept on her stomach beside Terry, her body relaxed and unguarded, one arm bent beneath the pillow, the other resting loosely at her side. Her breathing was slow and even, the deep, steady rhythm of someone fully surrendered to rest.

The thin blanket was draped low over her hips and legs, leaving her back bare, smooth skin catching the faint light of the room. Her shoulders were strong but soft, tapering into the gentle curve of her waist, the subtle definition of muscle visible even in stillness. There was a quiet power in her form, athletic without hardness, feminine without fragility.

Her hair, dark and textured, spilled freely around her head, slightly wild from sleep, framing the nape of her neck. The rise and fall of her back gave her an almost sculptural calm, as if the world had paused around her. She looked comfortable beside him, not posed, not self-aware, simply present, existing in that private, unobserved moment where vulnerability felt safe.

"Must've been a bad dream," he said aloud and to himself.

Terry then started stroking the sleeping beauty next to him, causing her to awaken, and she did so with a warm smile as she looked at him with soft brown eyes.

"Regine!" he called softly.

She turned her head to face him and stared softly at him just before closing her eyes again.

"Regine!" he called again.

The young lady then threw a pillow over her head.

"Regine! I got something for you!"

"I already had it," she said with a muffled sound from under the pillow.

Terry laughed.

Regine pulled the pillow off of her head and started laughing softly.

"You don't want me to go down on you?" asked Terry as she looked at him smiling.

"Well," she started, then she quickly threw the blanket off of her body revealing her soft brown skin and hourglass figure.

They both laughed.

"I take that as a yes," he said.

"That would be correct," she replied. "But I suppose you're gonna want me to do the same thing?"

"Well it is tit for tat, an eye for an eye, suck for a lick."

"If the shoes were reversed, would you suck my dick?" she asked.

"If the shoes were reversed, there would be no questions," he said gesturing like he just picked up something and started licking. "I would slob your knob so good, you would think I had a blow pop in my mouth."

She laughed. "Well get busy then!"

"Ooh a controlling freak," he said as he started kissing her. Terry then slowly started lowering himself gently over her body as he kissed her down the length of her frame.

As he hit her spot, Regine started moaning in ecstasy.

TWO

THE NEXT MORNING, the alarm clock went off again cutting the radio on and Terry immediately hit the top of it, silencing the clock while clumsily getting out of the bed and then walking across the hall from the bedroom towards the bathroom.

Terry stepped into the bathroom and pushed the door closed behind him.

The fluorescent light flickered once before settling.

He leaned forward toward the sink and stopped.

Something felt...off.

His stomach dropped, not sharply, but the way it does when an elevator halts between floors.

His heartbeat thudded once, hard, then again, faster.

The room felt warmer. Or maybe it was just him.

Terry swallowed and placed both hands on the edge of the sink, steadying himself.

The porcelain felt colder than it should have.

His breathing sounded wrong in his ears, too close, too loud.

He lifted his eyes to the mirror.

And screamed.

There was a topless woman in the mirror staring back at him, and it was her.

She screamed.

She then covered her breast. "No...No...This...this can't be right!"

She unfolded her arms and again got startled by her own full round breast. She screamed again and threw her arms back over them.

"Baby what's wrong?" called a male voice from inside Terry's bedroom.

Terry froze for a second. "Who's in there?" She then ran back into the room and saw a young chocolate complexioned brother in her bed.

"Yo...who...the fuck...are you?" asked Terry. "And where's Regine?"

"Who?" asked the young man. "You told me you ain't got no roommate?"

"No mutha fucker," started an angry topless Terry. "Who are you? And where's the girl I came home with last night?"

"Say what?" the man then shook his head. "I should've known somethin' was wrong with you...I'm Reggie! I came home with you last night. We met at Club Pegasus...remember?"

Terry lost her breath for a second. "We what?" asked Terry in disbelief of what she was hearing.

"We had a couple of drinks at Club Pegasus last night, you invited me back to your place, we talked for a little bit and then we..."

"It is so important for your health that you NOT finish that sentence!" scolded Terry.

Reggie stood up, revealing his naked self as the blanket fell off of him.

Terry covered her eyes and turned her head to the side. "Please sit down...and put that blanket over you!"

Reggie complied as he looked at Terry as if she were off her rocker. "Don't you remember waking me up and going down on me?"

Terry screamed. "No...that was not you, that was not you, that was not fuckin you!"

Reggie stood up while holding the blanket around himself as Terry started to cry.

"I am a fuckin' man," screamed Terry. "I have a dick..." she stopped as she looked down in her pants. "Had a dick. I brought a girl home last night and fucked the shit out of her!"

"I've been all around down there," replied Reggie "And there ain't NO evidence of a dick."

Terry started to bend forward. "No, this isn't happening this isn't happening."

Reggie smiled. "And I fucked the shit out of you!"

Terry stood up and walked quickly over to Reggie.

She then punched him dead in his mouth. "Get out, get out, GET OUT!" she yelled, as Reggie quickly started grabbing his clothes.

Reggie then ran into the bathroom and closed the door.

Terry started crying and then screamed again.

THREE

SHE WAS NOW wearing a pair of baggy denims, sneakers, and a sweater. Terry paced nervously through the apartment as she waited for her friends to show up. She kept checking her pants, especially her crotch, hoping that something would change and that she would find her prize possession, her manhood, in her pants.

Terry had been all through the apartment looking for some sign that she was indeed a man, but everything from her pictures to her clothing had been altered, as if to suggest, a man never lived in the apartment.

"This is a bad dream...this is a bad dream...this is a fuckin' nightmare!" she yelled angrily, out loud, and to herself.

She knew it was Jason's turn again to drive today so she never bothered to call them she just waited for her friends to show up.

If they all changed into females too, that would soften the blow, but somehow she knew, that wasn't the case.

A knock at the front door interrupted Terrys' pacing as well as her thoughts and she responded by quickly going over to the door and opening it.

Bernard, Greg, Guang, and Jason were all standing in the doorway.

Greg developed a nefarious grin on his face as Jason peeked in the doorway.

"Excuse me sis," started Jason as he looked at Greg and gave him a look of disapproval. "Is Terry here?"

Terry started crying like a baby and Bernard rushed over to console her.

"Don't worry baby," started Bernard, "you know he'll be back 'cause he left you in his apartment, though he should've been back from the gym by now..."

Terry pushed Bernard away. "It's me Bernie...I...am...Terry."

Greg busted out in laughter. "Cuz get the fuck outta here...you aint no damn Terry!"

Guang walked past her abruptly and started looking around the apartment for Terry.

"Yo Terry!" he called.

Bernard stepped in Terry's face. "Un...un...what'd you do with Terry?"

Terry turned around and threw her hands in her face as she groaned in frustration.

Greg immediately started looking at her ass.

"Nigga it's me...I woke up this morning lookin' like this," she said as she turned back to face the trio. "...I'm fucked. I can't go to work...I can't go to school. I ain't even gonna tell you about how my random shot experience went last night."

"It is you!" exclaimed Jason with a puzzled facial expression.

Greg pointed at Terry's breast and reached for them.

"Are those real?" he asked.

Jason smacked his hands.

Uncomfortable, Terry folded her arms over her chest.

Guang came running out of Terry's room. "Guys...She's in all of Terry's old pictures!"

Jason grabbed a gentle hold of Terry. "All right Terry...just calm down."

Terry pulled away from him. "Calm down...calm down? When you turn into a woman and I back into a man, then I'll calm down, but until then...I am not leaving this apartment."

She then plopped down onto the couch.

Jason nodded his head in agreement. "Cool...cool...and when your moms does her weekly check on your fridge today...you can explain to her..."

Terry jumped back up and grabbed the sides of her face and froze as if she were a small child who accidentally put aftershave on his face for the first time.

"Oh shit...my mother!"

Greg was still scoping out Terry's body.

Suddenly, a loud knock on the door caused everyone to look towards the door as if a ghost just announced its arrival in front of it.

"Yall didn't come wit anyone else...did yall?" asked Terry.

Bernard quickly shook his head in the negative.

Another knock on the door and then, "Terry it's me, open up! I came early because I misplaced my key!"

"Shit...it's my mother!"

Greg laughed. "Damn bro...I mean sis...you kinda fucked up."

"Don't let her in!" Terry whispered nervously.

Jason put his arm around Terry and walked her towards the door. "Listen Terr...whether this is temp or perm...you gonna need your moms...you can't just ignore her, and we'll help you figure out what happened."

Terry looked at Jason angrily.

"I think your mom is gonna notice the difference," said Greg.

Another loud knock at the door and Terry exhaled as she looked angrily at Jason.

"Terry baby," started her mother, "I know you're still here, I saw your jeep and Jason's Durango."

Terry walked over to the door and opened it, bracing herself and preparing for the worst.

Terry's mom, Mrs. Harper, walked in and kissed her on the cheek, apparently seeming to not notice the change.

"Sorry I came so early...but I'm gonna need your spare key in order to get back in after... I...go... shopping."

Mrs. Harper stopped talking and looked at Terry and her friends as if something was wrong and they all stood around, bracing themselves.

Terry approached her mother. "Mom I can explain...."

"You damn well better be able to explain this," interrupted Mrs. Harper angrily. "You mean to tell me, all of you were in here and not one of you could open the door for me?"

Terry, Greg, Bernard, and Jay all looked at each other with puzzled expressions on their faces.

"If Jay and Guang weren't here, I'd think yall were having some sort of sex fest going on in here," said Mrs. Harper.

"Excuse me?" asked Bernard.

"I'm sorry Bernie," started Mrs. Harper, "and Bernard, in fact Greg's the only one in here I don't trust."

Greg sucked his teeth.

"Jay don't let that fool corrupt you or my baby."

Jason looked at his friend and shrugged as Mrs. Harper turned and looked in the refrigerator.

"Yes maam!" said Jason.

Terry exhaled hard and headed into her bedroom to get her spare key.

She then returned and gave the key to her mother.

Mrs. Harper leaned into Terry. "You know...I really wish you'd stop hanging around all these boys... young men...except for Jay."

"Mom I..."

Mrs. Harper started looking through the cabinets. "I know...I know...mom they've been my friends forever...but this tom boy thing...it was cute when you were a little girl, but now it makes me think that you're a bit...dykish."

Mrs. Harper quickly turned to Bernard. "No offense Bernie."

Bernard developed a confused look on his face.

"None taken?"

Terry got in front of her mother. "Mom...just a minute ago you said I was capable of a ménage toi, now I'm being dykish?"

Mrs. Harper smiled as she touched Terry's face. "I'm sorry baby, I just want you to be a good example for Lena."

Mrs. Harper then closed the fridge and headed for the front door as Terry shook her head in the negative.

"You hurry up and get yourself to school...we're not paying your tuition so you can stay at home all day."

Mrs. Harper then left out of the apartment, closing the door behind her.

Terry then came out of the kitchen and grabbed her coat. "C'mon...I gotta get outta here!"

"You going to school?" asked Jason.

"You heard her!" said Terry. "Afterwards I'm gonna need a drink. I've gotta figure out what the hell's happening to me."

***

Terry walked in her class a few minutes late during her professors' lecture and scooted her way over to her seat. Her entrance briefly distracted the other students and the professor who glanced at her.

"Miss Harper?"

Terry faced her professor and stopped moving. "Yes?"

Professor Hart was a tall slender black man, chestnut brown in complexion, and older, only noticeable because his hair was all gray, as was his matching mustache and beard. He wore a blue dress shirt and black dress slacks with pleats in the front. He also wore black loafers.

"I would greatly appreciate it if you were able to arrive to class on time...thereby preventing yourself from interrupting my lecture."

"Sorry I..."

" ...Didn't ask for excuses," he interrupted. "Now find your seat quickly please."

Terry moved quickly to an open seat and sat down and then started opening her notebook.

"Now as I was discussing earlier, before I was so rudely interrupted..."

"And you just wasted another thirty seconds with that comment," blurted an irritated Terry.

"Excuse me Miss Harper?"

"And the name aint...Miss Harper...its Terry! T- E- R- R- Y...Terry."

"Well Terry...if you don't like how I conduct my class...you're more than welcome to leave."

"Since my classes are paid for...I'm just gonna be quiet and stay, thank you very much."

Professor Harts' eyes hardened. "Very well...as I was saying earlier...and you may want to jot this in your notes somewhere...blood is synthesized in the bones, more specifically, the flat bones and the long bones of the body...that would include...which flat bones Terry?"

Terry looked up from her notes somewhat surprised he had called on her.

"That would be...the bones of the sternum, the scapula, and the iliac crest, they make up the flat bones."

"Very good," he started, "the sternum, which is made up of the manubrium and gladiolus, and the iliac crest of the hip bone."

Marcus Smith, a young studious black man, raised his hand as Professor Hart acknowledged him.

"Yes Mister Smith?"

"What is the process of blood cell formation called?"

"That would be hemopoiesis," blurted Terry.

"I'm sorry Professor Hart...what is the process called? I was slightly distracted."

How dare he? She thought as her facial expression asked the same question.

"Hemopoiesis," replied Professor Hart as he glanced over in Terry's direction and then back at the young man, annoyed with the young man' obvious attempt to brown nose.

Marcus developed an embarrassed look on his face as Terry mouthed, *I told you so!*

The class went on for another forty-five minute and Terry took notes, and answered most of the questions in the class, causing Professor Hart to acknowledge her with a smile.

He was impressed.

Still upset about how the day started, she missed his look of admiration.

"For the next class," Professor Hart started, "I want you to study the rest of the section on the skeletal system and be prepared for a class discussion..."

The class getting up as a result of classical conditioning, as they recognized the lecture time was over according to their schedules, automatically interrupted the professor.

Professor Hart looked at his watch to confirm the time.

"And don't forget to do the review questions at the end of the unit... Miss Harp...Terry...can I see you for a moment please?"

As the class left and as Professor Hart placed his materials in his briefcase, Terry approached him.

"Professor Hart?"

"My apologies for coming at you during class," he started.

"No, I'm truly sorry professor...I had a really traumatic experience this morning, and I'm just ready to attack everyone."

"Looks like we both had a rough start to the day."

"You have no idea," she said.

"You're a very bright young woman, and you are always prepared when you come to class, if you have any problems and need to miss class, as long as it's not an exam day, just send me a message through the campus portal. I hope that you take care of your problems...I would hate to see anything hold an intelligent woman like yourself back from a successful future...we need more doctors you know."

"Doctor?"

"Think about the possibility, anyone who is as intelligent as you are and not afraid to stick up for him or herself, should lean in that direction."

The professor then left out of the class as Terry stood there smiling, briefly forgetting about her problems.

"Doctor Terry Harper," she started, "I like the sound of that!"

FOUR

"I'LL TAKE A strawberry daiquiri," said Terry as she passed her menu to the waiter.

At their favorite restaurant, T.G.I. Fridays on City Avenue, Terry, Jason, Greg, Guang, and Bernard met as they often did and sat at one of the big booth seats.

This time they were meeting because of Terry's current problem.

The atmosphere in the restaurant was always busy and there were often celebrities, athletes mostly, hanging out there.

Terry and her friends always picked this particular restaurant because they liked the sports entertainment on the various monitors throughout the restaurant, the menu choices and drinks available, not to mention it was the most convenient location for them all to meet at.

"Can I see some identification please?" asked the waiter,

Terry reached into her pocket and pulled out her drivers' license, glancing at it really quick to check her picture and seeing her feminine face on it. She then handed it to the waiter, who eyeballed it and then gave it right back to her.

"Thank you," he said. "I'll be right back with your drinks!"

"So as I started to say...this morning almost started off being problematic in class. But after I vented on and ranted against Professor Hart, everything else seemed to fall into place.

"That's nice," started Greg, "but you're still a girl."

"Woman," corrected Terry.

"You're pretty calm about this shit," started Guang. "I would be home putting on men's clothing, hoping I would just change back automatically."

"They're right Terry," started Jason, "We have to find Anna Homestead and get her to change you back before you end up stuck like this or something."

"Anna Homestead?" asked Terry. "Why Anna Homestead?"

"We think she might be behind why this happened to you," started Jason.

"You slept with her," interjected Bernard as the waiter returned with their drinks, "and humiliated her in public."

The waiter looked at Terry strangely as he sat everyone's drinks down and then quickly walked away.

"That was an asshole move on my part," admitted Terry. "But I refuse to believe this was Anna."

"Wait," asked Jason. "Do you like her?"

Guang smiled. "Shit he does!"

"Then why'd you treat her that way bro?" asked Jason.

"I dunno," started Terry, "defense mechanism, I guess. I'm not ready to give up who I am, and she was just pushing me in a direction I didn't want to go in."

"How could she push you in a direction you didn't want to go in?" asked Guang.

"She told me she was pregnant yo."

"Damn!" said Greg and Jason at the same time.

"What'd you say?" asked Jason.

"I basically told her a baby wasn't in my plans."

"Yo, that's fucked up," said Guang.

"Yeah, she definitely put the roots on you for that," replied Bernard.

"Naw he was right," started Greg, "'specially if he ain't want that shit!"

Jason pointed over to Greg. "See who you're thinking like now?"

"This is Karma in the worst way," said Guang.

"Well, I said what I said," replied Terry, 'besides, yall expect me to go to her lookin' like this?"

"Anyway," continued Jason as he shook his head in the negative, "she was the only one who we could think of, seems like with good reason now."

"I don't know what this is," started Terry, "but my chick hit list is too long for me to to try and figure out who did this. I just hope that whoever did this is getting her rocks off and will soon change me back."

Another waiter showed up with three bowls of soup and two salads and sat them on the table.

Greg sighed. "Well, it ain't right having a man's body one day and a woman's body the next."

The waiter looked strangely up and down at Terry.

"We are inclusive here and accept the trans community," said the waiter.

Terry shoed the waiter away. "All right...be gone!"

The waiter quickly rushed off.

What the...? she asked herself as she started looking around as if she was confused.

"What's wrong?" asked Bernard.

Terry looked down at her lap, "Did I?"

She put her spoon in her bowl. "Oh shit," she started as she put her hand over her mouth. "I think I'm leaking!"

"Like you pissed yourself or something," asked Greg

"I think I would've known if I had to pee!"

Greg chuckled. "I don't. know, that thang don't work like it used to."

Guang moved himself over to the left away from her.

"You on your period?" he asked.

The sound of forks and spoons dropping in the dishes at their table caused her to slightly tear up as she put her head down, embarrassed.

"Don't you have any feminine products in your purse?" asked Greg.

Terry lowered her voice to a whisper. "Why the fuck would I have feminine products when I was a man yesterday?"

Jason slapped Greg in the back of the head.

"Man, you got one more time to slap me!"

"What am I gonna do?" cried Terry in a low voice.

"Don't worry girl, "we got you started Bernard.

Jason grabbed his jacket and started to get up. I'm gonna run over here to the Target right quick and get you some products, a pair of pants, some undergarments, etc. When I get back, maybe you can see if one of the waitresses can help you out in the ladies room."

"I'll run wit you Jay," said Guang as he got up too.

"Thanks Jay, thanks G," Terry said softly. "Thank you too Bernie!"

"No doubt," started Bernard, "Friends for life, right?"

Jason and Guang both got up and left out of the restaurant.

***

Later in the restaurant bathroom, Terry locked the stall door and leaned her forehead against the cool metal partition.

Her hands were shaking.

She looked down at the unfamiliar item resting in her palm, its plastic wrapper crinkling loudly in the too-quiet bathroom. The stall felt smaller than it should have. The air smelled faintly of soap and disinfectant.

"Okay," she whispered to herself. "Okay... you can do this."

She peeled the wrapper open, then stopped.

The thing didn't make sense. Not really. She turned it over once. Twice. Her stomach twisted.

"I don't..." Her voice caught. "I don't know how this works," she said through the door.

A pause.

Then, gently, from the other side of the stall door.

"Hey. It's okay."

Terry flinched.

The waitress's voice was low, careful, like she already knew not to push.

"I've got time," the woman said. "You don't have to rush."

Terry swallowed hard. Her eyes burned.

"I was a guy yesterday," she said, the words tumbling out before she could stop them. "I mean, I *was*. I didn't wake up this morning thinking this was gonna be a thing I'd have to relearn in a restaurant bathroom."

There was no laugh. No shock.

Just a quiet, human pause.

"Yeah," the waitress said softly. "It can be hard to relearn stuff."

Terry let out a breath and stopped her legs from shaking.

"Can you...?" she asked. "Can you just, tell me one more time what I'm supposed to do?"

"Of course," the waitress replied. "Step by step."

Terry closed her eyes as the instructions
came, simple and calm and mercifully ordinary.

For the first time since changing, she felt
something loosen in her chest.

Not relief.

But survival.

FIVE

TERRY HAD SHOWERED after she returned to her apartment.

She didn't linger under the water. Didn't examine herself. Didn't try to understand anything she wasn't ready to name yet. She dried off, pulled on an oversized T-shirt. She then put on a pair of soft pajama pants she'd found shoved way in the back of her drawer, leftovers from a time when she used to wear pajamas, now unexpectedly useful.

Her apartment felt quieter than usual.

Not empty.

Just...observant.

She wasn't entertaining anyone like she had done prior to her transition.

She sat on the edge of the couch for a moment before reaching for the remote.

The television flickered to life, bathing the room in blue light.

A commercial played first, some perfume ad, slow and glossy, a woman moving through the frame like she knew exactly who she was supposed to be.

Terry snorted softly. "Must be nice."

She flipped channels.

"And let's talk about why you feel this way!"

Flip.

"You always want to make sure you add enough nutmeg..."

Flip.

"...oh Rose get a clue..."

Flip.

On the screen, a woman laughed, head thrown back, comfortable, she was unguarded. She wasn't performing. She wasn't trying to be anything.

She just *was*.

The woman on the television screen then submerged her whole head in the bathtub while smiling, her red hair floating on top.

She looked extremely happy.

Terry hugged a small pillow against her chest without realizing it and started watching the film.

Earlier that day, people had corrected her. Watched her. Helped her.

She hadn't hated it.

That realization landed heavier than anything else.

The TV droned on, the apartment humming quietly around her, and Terry realized she wasn't tired, not really.

She was alert.

Watching what was before her eyes.

Listening to the things she could hear.

Learning the lessons being taught through character interactions.

Whatever this was that was happening to her, she knew it wasn't over, not by a long shot.

***

Early the next morning she found herself at the gym and immediately noticed it smelled like disinfectant and rubber mats.

It wasn't a new smell, but for some reason, it was more noticeable today.

Terry stood just inside the entrance, adjusting the sleeves of the oversized gray sweatshirt she'd pulled from the back of her closet.

The pants were just as baggy, cinched tight at the waist, fabric pooling slightly around her sneakers.

She hated how visible she felt.

Not because the clothes showed anything, if anything, they hid too much, but because she was *aware* of herself in a way she'd never been before. Every step. Every shift of weight. Every bounce she hadn't quite learned to anticipate yet.

She scanned the room, then headed for a treadmill near the back.

Running had always helped. It was automatic. Mechanical. Something she could disappear into.

She started slow.

The belt hummed beneath her feet. Her breathing evened out. Music filled her ears, something aggressive and fast, something familiar.

For a few minutes, it worked.

Then she felt it.

A presence too close.

"Hey."

She ignored it.

"Hey, sorry," her neighbor on the treadmill leaned a little too much, "what're you listening to?"

She kept her eyes forward.

The guy leaned closer anyway. Mid-twenties. Tank top. Smiling like he thought he was doing her a favor.

She pulled one earbud out. "I'm busy."

"Oh, yeah, totally, I just…"

She turned her head, just enough to meet his eyes.

"I said I'm busy!"

He laughed, hands raised. "Okay, okay. Just saying hi…bitch!"

She looked at him as if he were crazy and then put the ear buds back in.

He didn't leave right away.

She turned the speed up.

Her focus shattered. Her rhythm broke. She became hyper-aware again, of her chest, of the way the sweatshirt shifted with movement, of the eyes that lingered longer than they should have.

Against her will, her eyes shifted around the gym.

Another guy smiled at her near the weight racks.

Someone else nodded.

Two guys near the stationary bikes were looking in her direction while nodding and slapping their hands as if some big plan was made.

She hit the stop button abruptly.

Screw this.

She grabbed her bag and left without cooling down, heart pounding for reasons which had nothing to do with exercise.

***

By the time she got back to her apartment, the irritation had settled into something heavier.

She showered. Changed into jeans and a loose sweater. Pulled her hair back and stared at herself in the mirror longer than she meant to.

She was still trying to reconcile the reflection with the person she remembered being.

The knock at the door startled her. She then heard her door opened.

"Terry!" her mother called. "We're here."

Her stomach dropped as she ran out of the bathroom to greet her parents.

She opened the door to find her parents smiling, her mother already stepping forward to hug her like nothing in the world had changed.

Her father followed, carrying a small bag of pastries. "I know you don't like carbs but, we brought breakfast anyway!"

And between them-

"Who are you?" her sister Lena blurted out.

Terry froze.

Lena stood there, twelve years old, backpack slung over one shoulder, eyes narrowed in open

46

suspicion. She stared at Terry's face, then her hair, then her clothes, as if trying to solve a math problem which refused to balance out.

Her parents didn't react.

"Sup munchkin," Terry said carefully, using a greeting she always gave her little sister.

Lena pointed at her. "You're not..."

Terry coughed loudly interrupting her. Another louder cough as she put her fist perpendicular to her mouth.

Her mother shot her a look. "Lena."

"What?" Lena asked still confused. "I'm just saying..."

"That she hates my hair like this," she interrupted. She then gave Lena the side eye. "You always find the most interesting way to criticize me."

Terry crossed the room quickly and crouched beside her sister, lowering her voice. "Can I talk to you for a second?"

Lena's eyes flicked between Terry and their parents, then back again. "Why are they acting like this is normal?"

Terry swallowed and in a low voice said, "Because... to them, it is."

"That doesn't make any sense."

"I know. Come on."

Terry's parents chatted in the kitchen, blissfully unaware, as if the air wasn't thick with unspoken truth.

She pulled Lena into the bedroom and closed the door. She then sat Lena on the bed.

Lena blinked. "You were my brother!"

"I still am," Terry said quietly. "Just... different."

Lena's face twisted, and she then looked her up and down. "I'll say. What happened?"

Terry paced in the room. "Honestly, I don't know...I fell asleep a man and woke up a few days ago... like this."

"They don't seem to know?"

Terry shook her head. "I know...I know, but I need it to stay that way until I can fix this."

"Why?"

"Because they don't need the stress and confusion I'm going through right now. And because I'm still figuring this out myself. As far as I know right now, only you and the fellas seem to be aware of who I was!"

"Not even at work or school?"

Terry shook her head.

"So far...no."

Lena studied her for a long moment. Too perceptive for her age. Then she said, "So right now you're, like... undercover?"

Terry almost laughed. "If that helps you deal."

Lena sighed dramatically. "You owe me, I mean really owe me."

"For what?"

"For not saying anything."

Terry smiled. "Fair."

"I want you to help me with math," Lena said immediately. "And you have to take me to the movies. And you can't be weird about it."

Terry nodded. "Long as the math ain't word problems cause I suck at those, but I'll try my best..."

Terry then extended her hand to Lena who shook it.

"Deal!" she said.

Lena leaned back, satisfied.

"Okay. I won't tell."

From inside the kitchen, her mother called, "Everything alright in there?"

"Yeah," Terry answered, voice steady. "All good."

Lena smirked at her. "She's teaching me about period stuff!"

Terry exhaled. "Please don't add anything extra."

Lena laughed.

The secret held. For now.

SIX

BY MID-MORNING, Terry was already tired.

Not the kind of tired sleep fixed. Not the kind that could be relieved with a hot cup of coffee with two cream and three Splenda.

It was the kind which lived behind her eyes.

She stood in line at the café, phone in hand, aware of the man behind her without turning around.

She felt him shift closer. Not enough to warrant a reaction. Just enough to notice.

She stepped forward anyway.

When she reached the counter, the barista smiled, warm, familiar, and Terry smiled back automatically. It came easy now. Too easy.

"Can I get..." she started.

The man behind her leaned around her shoulder. "She'll have whatever's quickest."

Terry blinked and turned around.

"I'm ordering," she said, not loud, not sharp.

The barista laughed awkwardly.

The man raised his hands in surrender, smiling like it was a joke, like she was cute when she corrected him.

Terry stared at him angrily and didn't smile back.

She turned back around. "As I was saying," she started. "I'll take a medium vanilla latte...please."

"Right away," responded the barista.

After getting her drink, Terry walked past the man and mumbled mockingly and dramatically, "she'll have whatever's quickest..."

The man shook his head in the negative as he stepped up to order.

Outside, the street felt louder than it used to. She caught herself adjusting her stride, slowing when someone passed too close, speeding up when footsteps lingered behind her.

She hated that she noticed.

She hated more that she remembered to notice.

At the crosswalk, a car rolled to a stop. The driver waved to her to cross the street with exaggerated politeness, smiling.

She nodded once and crossed quickly, heart beating faster than necessary.

I should've parked in the campus garage, she thought.

Nothing happened.

That was the point.

In class, she was more focused. She no longer lost time staring or chasing after the opposite sex, because she didn't want that, not now.

She stopped at the library and tried to find information on Voo doo, or witchcraft, hoping she could find her own answers regarding what happened to her.

She found information on theories and different cultures, but nothing on actual cases of people changing sexes or swapping bodies or anything of that nature.

As guys constantly approached her in the library, interrupting her focus, she grew tired and left the school, heading back to her car.

After getting to her car and driving off, she made her way down Spring Garden Street and then turned right on to Delaware Avenue in order to jump on I95 North, to go back home.

By the afternoon, as she got closer to home, her phone buzzed twice. There were messages from friends. There was a reminder about a group project for one of her classes. Then there was a text she didn't answer because she didn't have the energy to phrase her response carefully enough.

When messaging now, everything required phrasing now.

Then she saw a text of some random guy who enclosed a dick pic in the text message.

"Ew...gross," she said as she flipped the phone close and dropped it in the seat next to her.

By evening, she was home again.

She locked the door, leaned back against it, and exhaled.

Her apartment felt smaller than it had that morning.

She kicked off her shoes and sat on the couch without turning on the lights.

She then laid down while staring at the ceiling.

The phone rang, the land line.

She turned to the side and stared at it as it rung three times.

She then picked it up.

"Hello," she answered sleepily.

A pause.

She smiled a little as she then sat up. "Oh hey Bernie...whuz up?"

She paused for a minute as she listened.

She laughed a little. "I can't tonight, you know Wednesdays are my long days, I gotta work right after class tomorrow, but maybe Friday?"

She paused again as she started to nod in the affirmative as if anyone could see her. "Right, we can go to the usual spot. I guess while I got this hot chick thing going on, maybe...I'll try and find somethin' nice to wear."

A pause.

She laughed. "Is Lamar coming?"

She paused briefly.

"Well tell him if anything changes, he should come, shit...the more the merrier!"

She paused one more time. "It's cool, I'll holler at you Friday then. Aight...peace." She then hung up the phone and laid back down on the couch

The quiet wrapped around her, thick and welcomed, like a warm blanket.

She didn't feel sad.

She felt spent.

On the coffee table sat her keys, her cell phone, her purse and a notebook. Evidence of a life that hadn't stopped, only shifted.

Terry stared at her hands.

They felt like hers.

That part wasn't confusing anymore.

What confused her was how much effort it took to simply exist now.

She closed her eyes, not to sleep, just to stop processing.

For the first time, she understood something without needing to explain it.

Tomorrow would feel like this too.

And the day after that.

She just struggled with a few days and yet, somehow, women dealt with this every day and still showed up to life.

She yawned and stretched, arms all the way outward and up above her.

"I'm tired yo, fuck a shower tonight," she proclaimed out loud and to herself as she closed her eyes and yawned again.

Suddenly she opened her eyes and rolled them as she sucked her teeth.

"Awe shit," she started as she grabbed a tampon out of her purse. "This shit again, she said as she got up and headed quickly into the bathroom.

While in the bathroom, she turned the shower on.

SEVEN

ALMOST TO THE end of the week, Terry got tired of correcting people, so she stopped.

It wasn't something she did consciously.

It was not a planned decision.

It just... happened.

When the barista called her *ma'am*, without flinching, she answered.

When a cashier said *miss*, she nodded.

When a classmate asked if she needed help carrying her books or bags, she still said no, but said it much softer than she used to.

Each interaction left a residue.

There wasn't always anger.

There wasn't any fear.

But she did make her moves with calculation.

She started choosing where to sit based on who else was nearby.

She also started timing when she entered certain buildings and when she left them.

She started noticing reflections in glass before she noticed faces.

At work, her manager pulled her aside.

"You okay?" he asked. "You've been quieter lately."

Terry smiled automatically. "Just tired."

He nodded, satisfied.

Men always accepted tired.

In the bathroom, she caught herself adjusting her shirt before washing her hands. Checking behind her before turning around. Locking the stall even when no one else was inside.

That last one bothered her.

***

Later on that night, she stood in front of her mirror a little longer than usual. Not searching for answers, just taking inventory.

Her shoulders were less broad. Her hips, more pronounced.

The one that really annoyed her, was the way her posture had shifted without permission.

She tried standing the way she used to. She widened her stance. Then she lifted her chin. "Yo what up?" she asked herself while nodding in the mirror.

It felt... performative.

She let her posture drop.

Her phone buzzed.

A message from Jason.

> Jay: you alive?
>
> Jay: you been ghostin lately.

She typed, *yeah*.

Deleted it.

Typed, *busy*.

Deleted that too.

Finally:

> Terry: Just tired.

Told Bernie I'd meet you all down Club Egypt tmrw. Talk later.

She laid back on the bed, staring at the ceiling.

She wasn't losing herself.

She was becoming *aware* of how much of herself had always been wearing an armor.

EIGHT

FRIDAY MORNING ARRIVED quietly.

Too quietly.

Terry sat at her kitchen table with coffee she hadn't touched, watching sunlight crawl across the wall.

The week had been draining, and she decided to skip class today, her energy currency this week had been spent.

She'd spent the night dreaming in fragments, there were long hallways, strange voices, hands reaching towards her but never touching.

She thought about cancelling hanging with her homies as she sat on her bed contemplating her next move.

Her phone buzzed.

A message from Lena.

Lena: Mom says you're coming over later

Lena: also

Lena: don't freak out

Lena: but we need to talk

Terry's chest tightened. *Oh God.*

Terry: Mom lied.

Terry: Mtg w/ the fellas later

Terry: Will s/b before then.

Lena: Smiley face Heart emoji.

Terry fell back flat on her bed and forcefully exhaled.

***

Terry walked into the front door of her parent's house wearing low-rise, straight-legged black denims which hugged her at the hips. She also wore a fitted satin top with an above the waist black denim jacket. She opted to wear platform sandals as she had no desire to even attempt wearing heels. Her hair, in long curls, was parted on the left.

At her parents' house, everything was the same. The couch. The photos, except all the pictures of the male version of Terry Harper were replaced with Terry in her current state. She looked at pictures of herself as a young girl with curiosity. *At least I was cute,* she thought.

Even the way her father read the paper like the world hadn't changed, was the same.

"What up pop?" asked Terry as she slapped her dad on the shoulder and continued on into the kitchen.

Terry's father lowered the paper and slightly gave Terry the side eye without Terry noticing.

Terry walked into the kitchen where her mother was watching a small television while preparing dinner.

She walked up to her mother and kissed her on the cheek.

"Tryin' to guilt trip me into coming over by tellin' Lena I was coming?"

"Now why would I ever do that?" asked Mrs. Harper with a sarcastic tone in her voice. "Well don't you look nice!" she said warmly changing the subject.

"I'm meeting up with the fellas downtown!"

Mrs. Harper frowned her motherly frown. "The fellas, the fellas...why don't you ever hang out with the girls?"

"Mom I..."

"I know, I know...mom I get along better with guys than I do with other women, mom women are backstabbers, I just don't trust them."

"Do I say all that?" asked Terry.

"You say it all the time," replied Mrs. Harper. "Baby, you feelin' okay?"

"Yeah ma, I'm good," started Terry as Lena ran into the kitchen and grabbed Terry's arm.

"Lets go, I need to show you something," said Lena as she pulled Terry up the back steps from the kitchen.

"You know ma, I blame you for this!"

"I have no idea what you mean," laughed Mrs. Harper as she went back to her meal prep and television watching.

***

Lena waited until they were in her room and after she closed the door.

"You walk different," she said bluntly.

Terry blinked as she looked at the pictures of them in the room. "What?"

"You seem more cautious. like you think before you move now," Lena continued. "You didn't before."

Terry laughed softly. "What? You've seen me like three times since this started and you've already concluded that? You're imagining things."

Terry picked up a picture she remembered taking with her sister, she was in high school at the time, she definitely didn't have pig tails, but the girl in the picture had pigtails.

Lena shook her head. "No. You're... different."

That word again.

"Of course I'm different, I'm wearing a bra and panties when I never thought I would," said Terry as she showed the picture to Lena. "What do you see here?" she asked changing the subject.

"You and me," Lena said.

"I know that," she started sarcastically, "but what do I look like here?"

"My goofy brother."

"You see me as a boy here?"

"Of course, what do you see?"

"I see myself as a girl with pigtails."

Lena laughed as Terry returned the picture from where she got it.

"Not funny!" said Terry.

"But like I was saying, the way you act the way you move..."

"My mannerisms?" interrupted Terry.

"YES!" proclaimed Lena, "your mannerisms, you seem different."

"I'm tryin' to get used to moving around in this body."

"Well don't get to used to it," replied Lena, as obnoxious as he is, I still want my brother back."

"That's a big word for you," started Terry, "you think I'm obnoxious?"

"Yeah, well you were, but it's okay, I still love you." Lena hugged Terry.

Terry reciprocated. "I love you too munchkin!"

Terry then glanced at the clock in Lena's room.

"I better get goin'," started Terry, "you figure out what you wanted to see at the movies yet?"

"*Shrek,* it comes out next week, on the eighteenth," she said excitedly.

"Aight," started Terry, "*Shrek* it is! I'll let you know which day."

***

Friday nights usually meant noise.

There was always loud music.

There were always large crowds.

And there was always movement.

For Terry, Friday nights also used to mean, the reassurance of being able to be seen without the awkwardness of being evaluated.

Now, Terry stood down by the waterfront just outside Club Egypt, fingers curled tight around her keys, watching all the reflections on the door instead of the door itself.

She took a breath, grabbed the handle, opened the door and walked in.

The *'Thong Song'* by Sisco filled the club as most people danced.

Some stood at tall circular tables like the one Bernard, Guang, Greg and Jason were waiting for Terry at.

Bernard waved from over at the table, already laughing.

Inside, the air was thick, perfume, sweat, bass. It was the kind of place where close proximity was unavoidable.

A man brushed past her shoulder. He didn't apologize for it. He didn't even register he had done it.

Another man leaned too close when he spoke. He was too loud. He was too familiar.

"YOU GOT A MAN?" he asked, grinning, the smell of his fruity drink jumping off of him at the same time.

"RIGHT HERE," Terry said, pointing at Jason. She then waved to the man and mouthed the word, *bye!*

The man smiled wider.

"YOU WANT A REAL ONE?" he asked.

Terry stared at him. Not angry. Just tired.

"MY REAL ONE IS RIGHT HERE!" she said.

Jason nodded at the guy. Slid closer to Terry. He then wrapped his left arm around Terry's shoulders. And then signaled with his head for the guy to keep moving.

The man backed up, hands raised and moved on.

"Thanks Jay," she said lightly.

"No worries, we got you," Bernard said as Jason moved his arm from around Terry.

"So what's going on with you?" asked Jason. "You know we just as worried about all of this as you are."

"I highly doubt that," replied Terry. "None of you, not even Bernie, had to wait almost a whole week for a period to go away."

"Why you gotta say it like that?" asked Bernard with disappointment in his voice.

Terry frowned, catching herself, "You know, you're right, I'm trippin'...sorry guys...yall have always been there for me!"

"And that's never gonna change," said Guang.

"If anyone gives you static," started Jay. "You send them our way!"

"Damn straight," added Bernard.

Terry smiled. "Thanks guys."

***

Hours later and *This is How We Do It*' by Montell Jordan was now playing.

People were still dancing as if the night had just started.

In the bathroom, Terry stood at the sink washing her hands while another girl stood next to her and applied lip gloss.

"You okay sis?" asked the girl as she glanced over at Terry while puckering her lips.

"I'm good," she started, meeting her eyes in the mirror. "You?"

"You know how it is," she started, "everyone wants a piece of cake, but no one wants to bake it."

Terry chuckled. "Meaning?"

"You know," started the bathroom buddy. "I'm sure you know!"

Terry shook her head no, clueless.

"Men are always looking for the next great release! They always want to have sex wit cha, but never want to put in a little work to build a relationship."

"Yeah, but isn't that what yall...we want too?"

"Did you really just ask that?" started the stranger as she turned around and leaned her backside against the sink counter. "Who wants random funky men touching their body week after week? Or even night after night?"

Terry looked as if she were reflecting.

The stranger continued. "The party scene is good once in a while, but at the end of the day, I want someone who I can cuddle with, who will rub my feet and who I can share everything with...my mind, body, and soul."

"I guess I never gave that much thought," replied Terry.

The stranger then slowly made her way to the bathroom door and turned as she started to leave. "Then sis, you are a rare breed!"

She then left out.

"Huh," Terry said to herself. She then just looked at herself in the mirror for another minute before leaving out.

***

"I don't know," started Jason while shaking his head no, "honestly, I'd much rather focus on getting through school before I think about that commitment stuff."

"You can have both," started Bernard as Terry soon joined them. "I have both! I'm doing really well in school, Lamar and I..."

"Yo that is not the same thing," started Guang.

"Definitely not the same thing," added Greg, as Guang just looked at Greg with the *I can't believe we're agreeing* face.

"And why the hell not?" asked Bernard. "Is it because we're gay?"

"YES!" proclaimed Greg as Jason just shook his head in the negative.

"Yes," started Guang, "but I'm sure my reason for answering that way is much different than his," he added gesturing towards Greg.

"Do it explain," said Bernard as he gestured toward Guang with a hand.

"It's actually really simple," started Guang, "With you and Lamar, you only have to worry about you two...but if Jason were to commit with someone, and get her pregnant, a baby changes the whole game!"

"And on that note," interjected Terry, "I'm gonna head out!"

"You want us to walk you to your car?" asked Guang.

"No," I'm good, it's all good," she started, "Bernie, thanks I needed this!"

"It's all good," he said, "call me tomorrow!"

"Bye yall!"

They waved and she left."

"I hear what you're saying, "started Bernard as Greg watched Terry leaving.

"Yo, Imma go see if I can get a ride wit Ter, "interjected Greg. "I'll get wit yall."

"Alright Greg!"

"See ya Greg!"

Greg then left after Terry.

***

Terry left out of the club and crossed Delaware Avenue to get to her jeep. As she got close and pulled out her key, she was forced up against her jeep as her attacker had her pinned against the car.

"What you doin' all out here by yourself sweet thang?" asked the attacker as he held her tightly against the car while looking up and down at her body.

Although she struggled to free herself, Terry couldn't move.

"Please..." Terry started as the attacker held her tight against the car and rubbed the back of her ass with his crotch.

"Oh," he started as he took his free hand and reached for his zipper. "You want this d..."

A clunk on the head interrupted the attacker as he let go of Terry allowing her to turn around and see him fall to the ground.

Greg returned a gun to his waist band.

Nervous and with tears in her eyes, Terry hugged Greg tightly.

"Thank you, thank you," she said as she trembled a bit. "He was about to...he was about to..."

"I know," started Greg, "good thing I came out to ask you for a ride!"

"A ride?" asked Terry nervously, "I don't even think I can drive, " she said nervously as she looked down at her unconscious attacker. Then she looked at Greg and tapped him on the chest. "Greg, you can drive my car, can you drive me to my crib? You can crash on my couch."

"Ter...I don't know..."

"Please bro, I wouldn't normally ask you this but I'm just too shaken, I don't think I will make it home like this."

Greg started shaking his head,

"Okay Ter...okay. No worries." he said as he took her key and took her around to the passenger door of her jeep and opened it.

He held it open until she was all the way in.

Greg then closed her door and went around to the other side, stepped over the unconscious attacker, and got in.

They then drove off.

NINE

TERRY CAREFULLY CARRIED two coffees into the living room and sat them on the coffee table.

Greg writhed uncomfortably as he saw her breast and felt himself have an erection.

"I really need this," started Terry as she picked up her coffee and took a sip. I aint neva been in no situation like that."

"I'm glad I got there when I did," started Greg "And good thing I had my jawn on me too."

"I didn't even know you had a license to carry, let alone a gun. wait 'til I tell the fellas how you came to my rescue, maybe now they'll stop givin you shit."

"May...be," he agreed. "Hey...you said this jawn pull out into a bed?"

Terry put her coffee on the table after taking another quick sip.

"Um...,"she started as she positioned herself just in front of him and lifted the center pillow slightly off the sofa, then, "The handle is right here under the middle pillow, after moving them of course, just pull the handle straight out and you're good.

She then put the pillow back down as Greg, unknowingly to Terry, stared at her ass the whole time.

Terry turned back around and pointed to the small hallway where the bathroom and her bedroom were.

"You already know the washer and dryer are in the hall closet, in case you need to wash your clothes."

"Thanks Ter," said Greg.

"No, no, no," Terry started as she picked up her coffee, "Thank you for being my hero tonight."

She raised the cup about to drink.

"Blankets?" he asked. "

She quickly sat the cup down again.

Blankets," she said. "Knew I was forgetting something."

Terry took off towards her room.

Greg watched her to make sure she was out of sight as he pulled a metal flask an inch in length and an eighth of an inch in diameter out of his pocket. He didn't initially plan to use this on Terry, he was hoping to meet someone at the club who he could take advantage of, but right now he was hard with an erection and Terry looked better than a lot of the females he saw earlier in the night.

She is not supposed to remember if I do this right, he thought to himself.

He opened the container and poured a clear liquid into her coffee.

He then quickly put the flask back into his pocket and she came out twenty seconds later carrying a folded blanket, a folded sheet, and two pillows.

"There's a fitted sheet on the sofa bed," she started, "but you're more than welcome to sleep on the couch if you want. I have to take a hot shower after what happened tonight and then I'm turnin' in."

She went over to Greg and gave him a hug. "Thanks again."

She grabbed her coffee and went into her bedroom.

After a few moments, she then left out of her bedroom and went into the bathroom.

The shower was turned on.

Greg laid the blankets out on the couch, got under them, and grabbed a hold of his member as he waited.

***

Two hours passed and the apartment was pitch black and quiet.

Greg pulled the covers off and quietly got up and made his way in the dark to Terry's room.

He slowly inched open her door and was immediately excited to see that not only was she sound asleep, but she was topless. *She must have gotten hot and removed her shirt*, he thought.

Her breast sat out above her, bare and completely exposed.

He slowly started removing his tee shirt and boxer shorts and he then got into the bed next to her, but naked.

He started kissing on her and fondling her breast.

No response.

The mickey I slipped in her coffee must be working, he thought.

He then eased her undergarments off while watching her face and he then positioned himself under the blanket and on top of her as he realized, she was unable to resist.

***

Later in the morning, Terry sat on the floor next to the front door and had been crying for at least three hours, ever since she woke up and felt the pain below.

She didn't know how long he had been gone, only what he had done.

Terry now hated Greg and wanted to kill him.

She didn't know if she was too ashamed or too embarrassed to call the police, but she didn't.

She definitely wasn't going to call her parents for the same reason she didn't want to call the police. She didn't need to hear the *'I told you so'* comments of having all male friends.

Jason and Guang, though both sweet and supportive friends were straight males, and at the moment, they couldn't be trusted.

She suddenly jumped upon hearing a knock on the door.

She sniffled but didn't move.

Another knock.

"TERRY...OPEN UP ITS BERNARD!"

Terry jumped to her feet and unlocked the lock and pulled it open. As soon as Bernard

72

came in, she hugged him tightly and started crying harder.

"Bernie I...I want this to end! I can't do this shit anymore!"

"Shhh, " started Bernard, "We got you!" He said confidently knowing that Guang and Jason were already on their way to find Greg and to beat his ass!

TEN

THE ALARM CLOCK went off the next day at the usual time, but Terry was already out of bed, sitting at the kitchen table, drinking a cup of coffee.

'*One More Try*' by George Michaels was playing, already in the song.

♪That look in your eyes♪

♪is telling me, no♪

♪So you think that you need me♪

♪that you'll never leave me♪

♪I know you're wrong♪

♪I wrote the song♪

♪just let me go♪

As the song continued playing, she sat there and sipped long and hard on her coffee and thought about everything that's happened to her since she woke up as a female.

The last thing that happened was the one thing she never saw coming and something she never expected, not from someone she considered a longtime friend.

She sat the cup down, walked in the bathroom, and stared at herself in the mirror.

Her face was pale and told the tale of someone who had been crying. She never thought that she was looking at a total stranger any more than she was right now.

"WHAT...THE FUCK...DO YOU WANT FROM ME!" she yelled to her reflection.

She stared at herself as if she were expecting to get a response.

She looked over to her left and picked up a black porcelain liquid soap dispenser and threw it against the wall, shattering it as the soap which was contained within it started oozing down the wall.

Again, she stared into the mirror while her hands rested on the sink, eyes reddening, with a tear descending down the left side of her cheek.

"You, whoever you are, want me to suffer as a woman?" she asked no one in particular. "Well let me tell you! I am suffering! I AM SUFFERING! Are you happy?"

She stared again hard and started wiping the tears from her eyes. "ARE...YOU...HAPPY?"

She then started crying as she looked briefly down at the sink and then back up at the mirror."

She wiped any evidence of tears off her face and then straightened up a bit. "If this is what I have to be now, what I have to deal with...then so be it, but whoever you are...whoever is doing this...you will not take me away from me!"

Terry then walked out of the bathroom and went into her bedroom. She looked through her closet and found something to put on.

She then went back into the bathroom and started her shower.

***

The Sunday afternoon warm sunrays peeked through the mini blinds of her apartment as Terry paced back and forth like a nervous teenager.

She wore navy blue denims and a black tee shirt. Her hair was combed out into her normal long curls with the part on the top left-hand side. She had her black sneakers on.

The doorbell to her apartment soon rung and she nervously went over to the door and opened it.

Bernard, Guang, and Jason all stood in front of the door looking present. Not with smiles or angry faces, or looks of pity, just present, and that was what Terry needed right now.

They all came in and she directed them to the couch.

"Please have a seat," she said.

Guang sat in the middle and Jason was to her right and Bernard sat to her left.

"I'm sure...you are all aware by now of what happened..."

She paused.

"...of what Greg did to me. When I first realized what happened, I was ashamed, embarrassed, and afraid to tell anyone because I was like...I brought this on to myself...being friends with men as a woman...asking him to drive me here and without hesitation, letting him stay here...whatever...but I did nothing wrong...tears came out of her eyes...he violated my trust, and I will NEVER forgive him for putting me through that, and I swear to GOD if I see him on the street I am whoopin' that ass

on site! But what I am here to say to the three of
you now, is that...I'm not letting this claim
me...I am going to live every day with the belief
that I will be waking up as my genuine self
again, hopefully one day...SOONER RATHER
THAN LATER!" she shouted out to the
universe.

She then continued. "But I need to know
here and now if the rest of you are truly my
friends? Because I don't want to let the actions
of one asshole, determine how I treat the people
who truly love and respect me as I do them."

Jason stood up followed by Bernard and
Guang as they all moved around the coffee table
and went to embrace her.

Jason started, "Terry, no matter what sex
you are, we will always be your family!"

"Yeah we always got you!" exclaimed Guang.

"One hundred percent," added Bernard as
they all hugged her.

She hugged them back and teared a little.

Terry then pulled back. "I'm determined to
get my body back, no matter how long it takes
and I'm gonna need my boys!"

ELEVEN

THE THEATER SMELLED like butter and carpet cleaner.

Terry noticed it almost immediately, the way her stomach tightened as soon as they stepped inside. She told herself it was probably nothing, old building, stale air, nerves.

She bought the popcorn anyway because Lena wanted it, and she would share with her, because routines mattered.

Even though Lena knew her truth, this was supposed to be normal, in Lenas' words, she didn't want Terry to be weird about it.

They found their seats halfway down the aisle.

"You okay?" Lena asked, already stretching her legs towards the seat in front of her.

"Yeah," Terry said automatically. "Just tired. Long week with finals and all."

The previews started. As usual they were loud. The screen was too bright. Terry never noticed before how incredibly loud it was in the theater when the previews came on. She wondered if she was just becoming too sensitive when focusing or thinking specifically about the lights and the volume.

By the time the lights dimmed, the nausea had set in low and heavy, like a stone.

Terry started shifting in her seat, crossing and uncrossing her legs, pressing her palms into her thighs.

She then focused on Lena.

Being a child, Lena was laughing too hard at a joke that wasn't, in her opinion, that funny. Lena then nudged her arm.

"You know Mike Myers from *'Austin Powers'* is playing Shrek? And Eddie Murphy from *'The Nutty Professor'* is playing Donkey?"

Terry smiled? "Really?" She didn't care.

Lena continued whispering commentary like she always did, narrating and translating as if Terry wasn't watching the movie with her.

For a few minutes, the distraction worked.

Then the wave hit.

The increase was sudden.

It then hit her again, and again, relentless.

Terry swallowed and felt her throat with a slight burn.

"I'll be right back," she said, already standing.

Lena looked up, confused. "What?"

"Gotta go run to the little girls' room," Terry added quickly. "Don't move, I'll be right back."

She walked fast, but not too fast, moving from the middle to the end of the crowded aisle, past knees and coats and whispered complaints. She then headed up the side of the aisle to the exit.

Out the theater.

Across the lobby and as soon as the bathroom door swung shut behind her, she lost the fight, barely making it to the sink.

Her body folded forward as if it had decided to empty before she had.

Immediately the retching came hard and empty at first, then bitter. She gripped the edge of the counter, slowly breathing in through her nose, and exhaling through her mouth, her eyes were watery.

When it passed, she stood there, shaking.

She rinsed her mouth. Grabbed a paper towel and pressed it to her lips.

She then looked up.

The mirror showed her something pale and unfamiliar.

"You're fine," she whispered. "Get it together."

She splashed water on her face, grabbed another piece of paper towel, and forced her shoulders back before walking out.

Lena didn't say anything when she returned. She just leaned closer, her shoulder warm against Terry's arm.

That almost broke her, she needed it.

TWELVE

THE RESTAURANT WAS loud in a way that used to energize her.

Now it just made everything feel closer.

They were halfway through the appetizers when Terry felt it again, the same rolling pressure, the same warning heat crawling up her spine.

"So is everyone registered for next semester yet?" asked Guang.

"Chile I got two classes I have ta wait for someone to drop," said Bernard.

"Me too," said Jason as he noticed a discomforting look on Terry's face."

She set her fork down slowly.

"You good?" Jason asked.

Terry nodded too quickly. "Yeah. Just...give me a sec."

She stood, already regretting it.

She moved quickly.

The bathroom was at the back, past the restaurant kitchen. She barely made it inside before locking herself into a stall and dropping to her knees.

This time there was no mistaking it.

Her body took control and emptied violently and unapologetically.

When she finished, she stayed there longer than necessary, forehead resting against the cool metal partition, another unflattering position she never thought she'd be in, breathing through the aftershocks.

Something was wrong.

Not emotionally wrong.

Something was physically wrong. She couldn't remember eating anything that would have given her food poisoning, yet she has been sick for a few days now, there was no denying that.

When she returned to the table, Bernard was watching her carefully.

"You look green," he said gently.

"I...," she paused as she sighed. "I am fine," Terry said, but the words didn't quite carry the convincing tone they used to.

Guang tilted his head. "You've been saying I'm fine a lot."

"What's wrong with that?" she asked.

"You normally say I'm cool," he said.

Silence stretched.

Jason leaned back in his chair and took a breath. "Okay, I'm gonna ask something, and I'm not trying to freak you out."

Terry's chest tightened. "Then don't ask."

"Ter," Bernard said softly, "have you taken a pregnancy test?"

The question landed like a dropped glass.

She laughed once. Sharp. Disbelieving. "That's not, no. That's not what this is."

Jason didn't argue. Neither did Guang.

"I think I got a little food poisoning the other day," she added.

Bernard reached across the table, palm open. Not touching her. Just there.

"You've been sick more than a week now, and after everything that's happened…" He stopped himself. "I think it's at least worth knowing."

Terry pushed her chair back.

"I can't," she said teary eyed. "Not right now."

"No one's saying right now," Guang said quickly. "Just, soon."

She nodded as she wiped a tear from her eye, more to end the conversation than because she agreed.

***

Later that night, alone in her apartment, the thought wouldn't leave her.

She stood in the bathroom, staring at the cabinet under the sink.

The package she picked up on the way home the day before sat in there, because she had been wondering if that was the issue too.

She didn't open it.

Not yet.

Her hand rested against her stomach instead.

For the first time since everything changed, the fear she was experiencing wasn't abstract. It now had weight.

THIRTEEN

THE PHARMACY WAS brighter than it needed to be.

As she didn't want to be there, Terry noticed it immediately.

From above the fluorescent lights hummed softly and showing the aisles were too clean and too exposing for her liking.

As if she were a celebrity, Terry kept her head down as she walked past the cosmetics aisle, past the seasonal aisle, and went straight to the back.

She already knew exactly where they were. She purchased one on a prior stop and now she needed another one for confirmation.

She stood in front of the shelf staring longer than she meant to, pretending to read labels she didn't need to read.

There were different brands all with different promises. *Now with early detection. Find out fast with digital results.* And her favorite, *New and Improved.*

Her stomach rolled again.

Stop, she told herself. *You're not even sure.*

She grabbed the first box within reach and didn't look at it again until she was at the register.

The cashier didn't bother glancing at the item. Didn't pause. Just scanned it like it was gum or batteries.

That almost made it worse.

Back in her apartment, Terry set the bag on the counter and stared at it like it might move on its own.

She didn't take the test right away.

Instead, she sat on the edge of the bathtub with the lid closed, her elbows were on her knees, fingers laced together so tightly her knuckles ached.

Her body felt so unfamiliar lately and more unfamiliar with each passing day. Not hostile. Just...unrecognizable.

She pressed her palm flat against her stomach again, much slower this time. Not checking. Just grounding.

This isn't possible, she thought again, but the words didn't land the way they had before.

Eventually, she stood.

The box felt heavier than it should have when she opened it. Instructions folded neatly inside. Simple. It was too simple for something that could rearrange her entire life.

She set everything on the sink.

And then she stopped.

Her hands were shaking.

"Not yet," she whispered, not sure who she was talking to.

She put the test back in the box, slid it under the sink, and sat back down on the tub.

The nausea didn't come this time. *Maybe the first one was a mistake,* she thought.

She felt calm.
For some reason, that scared her more.

FOURTEEN

TERRY DREAMED SHE was standing in a long hallway.

Every door was closed.

As she looked at each and every door, she knew, somehow, that behind one of them was the answer. Not just to the question everyone had started asking, but to the one she hadn't let herself finish yet.

She woke before she opened any of them.

Morning light crept through the blinds, pale and hesitant. Her body felt heavy, like she'd been carrying something all night without realizing it.

The first thing she noticed was the quiet.

Again, this morning, no nausea. No wave of illness. Just a strange, suspended stillness.

She got out of bed slowly, half-expecting the room to tilt.

It didn't.

In the bathroom, she caught her reflection and paused.

She didn't look sick.

That thought brought no relief.

Her gaze drifted to the cabinet under the sink.

She opened it.

The box was still there.

She took it out and placed it on the counter again, more carefully this time, afraid if she were too rough, it might bruise.

Her phone buzzed on the bathroom counter. She picked it up and flipped it open.

A text from Bernard.

Bernard: You okay this morning?

She stared at it, then typed.

Terry: Yeah. Just tired.

The lie felt thinner now.

She flipped the phone closed and laid it down.

Her focus was on the box.

"This doesn't define me," she said aloud, the words sounding strange in such a small space. "Whatever it says."

She followed the instructions of the test mechanically, step by step. She didn't rush. She didn't stall.

When she was done, she set the test on the edge of the sink and turned away.

Thirty seconds.

She paced the length of the bathroom. Once. Twice. Her heart beating too loudly in her ears.

She turned back.

The result was already there.

Clear.

Unarguable.

Her breath left her in a slow, uneven exhale as she sank onto the floor, back against the cabinet.

"No," she whispered, not in denial, but in disbelief. Like the word itself might change something if she said it gently enough.

Her hand moved to her stomach again, instinctive now. "Why is all this happening to me?" she asked tearfully to no one in particular.

Obviously, no answer came.

Terry closed her eyes.

The fear was still there.

But beneath it, something else stirred.

Not joy. Not certainty.

Just the undeniable knowledge that nothing would be simple again as long as she had this body.

FIFTEEN

THE WAITING ROOM was too quiet.

Not peaceful, just muted, like sound had been wrapped in cotton.

Terry sat in a stiff plastic chair with her purse clutched in her lap, knees pressed together, eyes fixed on a faded poster of the female reproductive system on the wall across from her.

She didn't like looking at it.

She didn't like knowing the fact that she had everything shown on that wall.

Her foot bounced despite her effort to keep it still. Every few seconds, she checked the hallway leading back to the exam rooms, half-expecting someone to call her name wrong. Or worse, too loudly.

A nurse stepped out.

"Terry Harper?"

Terry stood immediately.

"Yes."

The nurse smiled politely and she seemed professional and neutral.

"Right this way," she said.

Terry followed her down the corridor, heart pounding harder with every step.

Please be a woman, she thought. *Please.*

The nurse led her into a small exam room and gestured toward the scale. "Shoes off please."

Terry complied, eyes down, movements careful. Everything about her body felt exposed lately, even when fully dressed.

After taking her vital signs, the nurse handed her a thin paper gown.

"You can change from the waist down. The doctor will be in shortly."

Terry nodded.

As soon as the door closed, she exhaled shakily.

The exam room was smaller than the waiting area, enclosed and quietly intimate.

The door was closed but Terry could hear the distant sounds of phones and murmured voices outside.

Overhead, the lights were bright but diffused, softened by a pale plastic cover which kept the room from feeling harsh.

The walls were painted a gentle beige, even toned all through the room, and decorated with more cross sectioned pictures of women's bodies, one pregnant, one not.

A faint scent of antiseptic lingered, clean and sharp, layered beneath something sweeter, meant to make the space feel less intimidating.

In the middle of the room was the exam chair which was sort of perpendicular to the door and covered with crinkling paper covering, which was printed with tiny baby bottles.

A step stool rested beside it, metal legs cool and scuffed.

The paper rustled at the slightest touch and movement, loud in the otherwise quiet room.

She quickly removed her clothing and changed into the gown and carefully folded her clothing and placed it in the chair next to the exam table.

She then got up and sat on the edge of the exam table, the paper crinkling beneath her, hands gripping the sides like it might slide out from under her. Her breathing grew shallow.

You can do this, she told herself. *This is medical. This is necessary.*

A knock.

"Come in," she said nervously.

The door opened.

And relief hit her so hard it nearly made her dizzy.

A woman stepped in. She appeared to be in her mid-forties with calm eyes and dark hair which pulled back neatly. There was no rush with her movements.

"Good morning," she said, offering a small, reassuring smile. "I'm Dr. Alvarez."

Dr. Alvarez carried herself with the quiet confidence of someone who had delivered difficult news and hopeful news in equal measure. Her dark hair was drawn into a low, practical knot at the nape of her neck, not styled for impression but for function. A few faint lines framed her eyes, not from stress, but from years of steady focus and patient listening.

She wore a crisp white coat over soft blue scrubs, her name embroidered in careful stitching above the breast pocket: Dr. M. Alvarez, MD.

A black stethoscope rested lightly and cleanly around her neck, not as decoration, but as a tool she had used hundreds of times with measured precision.

Her affect or expression wasn't overly warm, nor distant. It was centered. Grounded. The kind of face which invited honesty without demanding it.

When she spoke, her voice was low and even, shaped by patience rather than authority.

She didn't hover. She didn't overwhelm the room with medical jargon. She took her seat deliberately, making eye contact first, ensuring that whoever the person in front of her was, she felt seen before examined.

There was something Terry felt was steady about her presence, the kind of steadiness which made the sterile exam room feel, for just a moment, less intimidating.

Terry nodded quickly. "Hi."

Dr. Alvarez sat on the rolling stool, glancing at the chart. "I understand you're here to confirm a pregnancy?"

Terry swallowed. "Yes."

"And this is your first visit with us?"

"Yes."

"Is this your first pregnancy?"

"Definitely a yes," Terry replied.

"Okay," the doctor said gently, finally looking up at her. "Before we begin, I want you to know, you're in control here. If at any point, you're uncomfortable, we stop. We talk. Nothing will happen without your consent."

Something in Terry's chest loosened.

"Thank you," she said quietly.

Dr. Alvarez then paused, studying her more carefully now. Not clinically, attentively.

"Is there anything I should know before we continue?" she asked.

Terry hesitated.

Then, barely audible she said, "I've been through...something."

Dr. Alvarez nodded once. No questions. No pressure.

"Understood," she said. "We'll go slow."

The exam itself was awkward, uncomfortable, but not painful. Terry focused on breathing, on the ceiling tiles, on the sound of the doctor's voice explaining each step before it happened.

When it was over, Terry sat back up, heart still racing but intact.

Dr. Alvarez removed her gloves and met Terry's eyes.

"The test was accurate," she said. "You are pregnant. Very early."

The words settled heavy in the room.

"How far?" Terry asked.

"Based on what we're seeing? A few weeks. but, we'll need follow-ups to be precise."

Terry nodded numbly.

Dr. Alvarez continued, "Physically, everything looks normal. Given what you have shared, though I strongly recommend counseling support alongside prenatal care."

Prenatal.

The word made Terry flinch.

"I'm not...I'm not sure what I'm going to do," Terry said.

"That's okay," the doctor replied evenly. "You don't have to decide anything today. My job is to give you information and keep you safe."

Safe.

Terry absorbed that word carefully.

Dr. Alvarez handed her a packet of paperwork. "Take this home. Read it when you're ready. And Terry?"

"Yes?"

"You're not weak for feeling overwhelmed. What you're dealing with is real."

Terry nodded, throat tight.

When she left the office, sunlight hit her face harder than she expected. She stood on the sidewalk for a moment, clutching the folder to her chest, breathing in the city air.

A tear descended her left eye.

"Get it together Terry, she started out loud and to herself. "You're gonna wake up as yourself any moment now!"

Her phone buzzed.

A text.

Bernard: You good?

She stared at the screen.

Then typed: I don't know yet. But I will be.

She slipped the phone back into her purse and started walking.

SIXTEEN

THE APARTMENT FELT too small again.

Terry paced back and forth between the couch and the kitchen breakfast bar, arms folded tight across her chest.

Bernard sat at the table in the kitchen, elbows resting on his knees.

Guang leaned against the wall, quiet but alert.

Jason stood by the kitchen window, staring out at nothing in particular.

No one rushed her.

That made it harder.

"So," Jason finally said, turning back towards her. "You went to the doctor."

Terry nodded. Once.

Bernard exhaled slowly. "Okay."

There were no gasps.

There were no sounds of panic.

There was just an acknowledgement of the gravity of the situation.

"I'm pregnant," Terry said. Saying it out loud still felt strange, like she was borrowing someone else's words.

Guang straightened. "Confirmed?"

"Yes."

"How far along?" Bernard asked gently.

"Early. Real early."

Jason ran a hand over his face. "Damn."

Terry stopped pacing. "Don't do that."

"Do what?"

"Make it sound permanent."

Silence followed that.

Bernard tilted his head. "Ter… talk to us."

She hesitated, then dropped onto the arm of the couch, hands gripping her thighs. "I don't think this is going to last."

All three of them just looked at her.

She reacted to their expressions.

"I mean it," she continued quickly. "Whatever this is, the spell, the curse, the bullshit that turned my whole life upside down, it didn't start natural, and it's not going to end natural either."

Guang crossed his arms. "You have no idea what's going on!"

"I can feel it," she snapped. Then softer, "I've always felt it."

Jason watched her carefully. "So, you're saying you don't think you need an abortion?"

Terry shook her head. "No. I don't. Because I don't think it'll even get that far."

Bernard leaned back in his chair. "That's a big gamble."

"I know," she said. "But it's my body."

No one argued that.

Jason cleared his throat. "Okay. Then the next problem."

She knew what was coming.

"Your parents," he said.

Her jaw tightened immediately. "I don't even know if they need to know."

Guang blinked. "Ter…"

"They don't!" she insisted.

She got back up and started pacing again.

She then looked at Bernard. "Not yet. Not unless this pregnancy actually becomes something permanent…which I am sure it won't."

Bernard nodded slowly. "But if it does and they find out…"

Terry interrupted by laughing once, bitterly. "What am I supposed to tell them? That I don't know who the father is? That I got pregnant in a body that isn't even mine?"

Jason stepped forward. "You wouldn't have to."

She looked at him.

He held her gaze. Steady. Serious.

"I'll say it's mine."

The room froze.

"What?" Bernard said sharply.

Jason shrugged. "It makes sense. We're close. We hang out all the time, have for years. It wouldn't shock anyone at all not really…not even them."

Terry stood up immediately. "Absolutely not."

"Ter…"

"No," she repeated. "I am not letting you put that on yourself."

"It's not a big deal," Jason said. "It's just words."

"No, it's not just words," she shot back. "You don't get to sacrifice yourself because my life is screwed up."

Guang looked between them. "He's offering because he cares. We all do!"

"I know that, I do...I know," Terry said, voice cracking despite herself. "And that's why I can't let you."

Jason softened. "Look, I'm not saying we tell them tomorrow. I'm just saying, if it comes to it, you won't be alone."

Bernard stood and walked over to her, resting a hand on her shoulder. "No matter what happens, we'll figure it out together."

Terry closed her eyes for a moment.

"I don't want this to define me," she said quietly while tearing. "I don't want this to become who I am."

Guang nodded. "Then we don't let it."

She looked at each of them in turn.

"Give me time," she said. "That's all I'm asking."

Jason smiled faintly. "You got it."

For the first time since she left the doctor's office, Terry felt something settle inside her.

Not certainty.

But support.

And for now, that was enough.

SEVENTEEN

SEPTEMBER QUICKLY ARRIVED without asking permission from anyone.

Terry noticed it in the air first, the shift from heavy and humid summer heat to something sharper, unsettled. She sat at her small kitchen table in loose sweatpants and an oversized hoodie, laptop open, coffee gone cold beside her.

Online classes had started at the end of August.

At first, she told herself it was temporary. Just until things *"sorted themselves out."* Opting to avoid taking another biology, physics or even any chemistry courses because those courses required a lab. Taking a lab meant having to go in and she didn't want to do that, not with being several months pregnant.

Five months to be exact.

Living somewhere between denial and acceptance, her hand rested on the curve of her stomach, absentminded now. There was no hiding it anymore. Not from herself.

The screen froze during the video playing from her online course.

"...as we'll see in chapter..."

The audio cut out.

Terry sighed and slapped on the side of the computer several times.

Nothing.

Her internet had been acting strange all morning. Pages were loading halfway or not at all. Messages were being delayed. Error notifications were popping up and disappearing like ghosts.

"Of course," she muttered.

She leaned back in the chair carefully and shifted her weight. Her back ached more than it used to. Everything hurt more than it used to.

She checked her phone.

No new texts from Bernard or Jason. That was unusual.

She glanced at the clock.

8:46 a.m.

The TV was off. She hadn't turned it on yet. She preferred the quiet lately, it gave her the illusion of control.

Her phone buzzed suddenly.

A text.

Lena: Turn on the TV.

Terry frowned.

Terry: What?

The reply came slower than usual.

Lena: Just turn it on.

A knot formed in her chest.

She reached for the remote and clicked the television on.

The image was chaotic. Smoke. A skyline she recognized instantly even though it wasn't hers.

New York.

A reporter's voice cracked as they spoke, words tumbling one over another, *plane crash, tower hit, accident, unconfirmed.*

Shocked, Terry stood up a little too fast and immediately regretted it, one hand gripping the back of the chair as she steadied herself.

"What...?" she whispered.

She sank back down slowly; eyes locked on the screen.

Another camera angle. Another point of view on screen. People running. People screaming. Ash falling like snow.

Her phone buzzed again. And again.

Texts came in and out of order.

> Bernard: You seeing this??
> Jason: Ter u home??
> Guang: Stay inside. Don't go anywhere.

The footage cut to a wider shot just as the second plane hit.

Terry gasped sharply, one hand flying to her mouth, the other instinctively to her stomach.

"Oh my God..."

She sat there, frozen, as the world changed in real time.

The internet cut out completely.

The screen stuttered, then went black.

"No, no, no," she said, hitting the remote, then the laptop. Nothing.

Her phone still worked, but barely. Messages delayed. Calls failing.

She tried to call her parents.

No answer.

Her chest tightened, not panic exactly, but something close to it.

She hadn't spoken to them properly in months. She had been dodging calls. She cancelled visits, promised "soon" every time.

She looked down at herself.

At the curve she could no longer deny.

At the body that still didn't feel like home.

A knock came to the door.

Sharp. Insistent.

Terry jumped.

Another knock, harder this time.

"Terry!" her mother's voice called out. "Open the door!"

She lost her breath.

Her parents.

Here.

Now.

She stood up slowly, her heart pounding, every excuse she'd rehearsed evaporating at once.

Outside, the world was unraveling.

And inside, the one conversation she had been trying to avoid was finally waiting on the other side of the door.

EIGHTEEN

THE DOOR CLOSED behind them with a dull, final click.

For a moment, no one spoke.

Terry's mother stood angrily almost guard-like just inside the apartment, purse still clutched tight against her side, eyes scanning the room the way mothers normally do when they think something is wrong with their children, checking for danger or disorder. Looking for answers.

Her father lingered a step behind her, his jaw set, shoulders tense.

"Terry," her mother said carefully. "Why didn't you tell us?"

Terry swallowed. "I was going to."

"When?" her father snapped. "After the baby was born?"

The word hit the room hard.

Her mother's eyes dropped to Terry's stomach as tears welled in her eyes.

The silence that followed was thick, almost suffocating.

Mrs. Harper pressed a hand to her mouth, upset and in disbelief that her daughter would keep something like this from her.

Her father's face darkened immediately.

"How far along?"

"Five months," Terry said quietly.

"Five...five months" he repeated, in disbelief. "You've been hiding this for five months?"

Terry folded her arms over herself, instinctive as she turned and moved towards the kitchen.

"I wasn't hiding. I was... dealing."

"With *what*?" he demanded. "Because last I checked, you weren't seeing anybody."

She hesitated.

Just a fraction too long.

"It's Jason's," she said.

The lie came out smoother than she expected. Like it had been waiting.

Her father's head snapped up. "Jason?"

"Yes," she said quickly. "We were... together. For a minute."

Her mother looked between them, confused but processing. "Jason... your friend Jason?"

"Yes."

Her father took a step forward. "That boy been coming in my house, sitting at my table, eating my food and smiling in my face, knowing he's been having sex with my daughter and now he got her pregnant?"

"Dad..."

"Oh, I'm gonna have words with him," he said sharply. "Man-to-man words."

Terry's heart jumped. "No. No, that's not necessary I got this."

"Not necessary?" he scoffed. "He thinks he can just..."

"Dad!" she snapped, louder than she meant to. She took a breath. "Please. Just don't!"

He stared at her, surprised.

"This...it's, everything is already complicated," she continued, forcing her voice to stay steady. "I don't need things to get any worse."

Her mother finally found her voice. "Is he... involved?"

"Yes," Terry said, nodding. "He is abreast of everything. He wanted to tell y'all, I asked him not to, he is respecting my wishes. He's supportive."

That part wasn't a lie.

Her father looked away, rubbing a hand over his face. "Unbelievable."

The television suddenly caught his attention.

Smoke still billowed from the screen.

"What the hell is going on?" he muttered.

Terry's mother turned fully toward the TV now. "Is that New York?"

"Yes," Terry said softly. "Something happened this morning. The internet's been down. Phones are barely working."

Her mother's eyes widened. "Lena."

Her father straightened instantly. "She's at school."

"We need to go," Mrs. Harper said, already moving toward the door. "Right now."

Her father paused, looked back at Terry. The anger was still there, but something else had crept in right underneath it. Fear. Helplessness.

"We're not done with this," he said. "Not by a long shot."

"I know," Terry replied.

Her mother then stopped in the doorway and turned. She hesitated, then crossed the room and pulled Terry into a tight hug.

"We'll talk later," she whispered. "You hear me?"

Terry nodded against her shoulder. "I hear you."

The door closed again moments later, their footsteps fading up the hallway steps.

Terry stood there for a long second.

Then she exhaled.

Long. Shaky.

Her knees weakened and she sank onto the couch, one hand on her stomach, the other rubbing her temples.

"Jesus," she murmured.

Her phone buzzed.

She picked it up and typed quickly before looking at any received messages.

Terry: Heads up. I told my parents the baby is yours. They're heated. I stopped my dad from coming at you, but just... be ready.

She stared at the screen, waiting.

A reply came through a moment later.

Jason: I got you. Whatever you need. We'll deal with it.

Terry leaned back, closing her eyes.

On the television, sirens wailed.

Inside, for the first time all day, she felt something close to relief, despite everything else that was going on in the world.

It wouldn't last and she knew that.
But for now, it was enough to breathe.

108

NINETEEN

THE TELEVISION WAS cut on after they got home.

Mrs. Harper dropped her purse on the chair by the door and turned the volume up without thinking. Smoke filled the screen. A reporter stood stiffly in front of a skyline that didn't look real anymore.

Planes. Towers. Missing people.

Her husband stood with his hands on his hips, staring like if he watched long enough, the events which occurred might change.

"They say the Pentagon too," he muttered.

Mrs. Harper shook her head slowly. "Jesus!"

They stood there for several minutes, saying nothing. Just watching the same footage loop, the same words repeated, each time sounding less believable.

Finally, he clicked the TV off.

The silence that followed was heavier than the noise had been.

"Where's Lena?" he asked.

"In her room," Mrs. Harper replied. "Soon as she got in, she went straight there."

He nodded. "Good."

They moved into the kitchen without another word. Habit. Familiar ground.

Mrs. Harper opened the fridge and stared inside without really seeing anything.

"Five months," she said quietly.

He leaned against the counter.

"Five damn months."

"She didn't tell us because she was scared," she said. "You know that? You saw her."

"I saw her," he agreed. "And I heard a boy's name come out her mouth who I no longer trust."

"She panicked," Mrs. Harper replied. "And truthfully, if it would be anyone, I'd rather it be Jason than any of those other knuckle heads out there."

He rubbed his jaw. "I know, I know, but Jason or not, she's pregnant and she hid it from us."

Mrs. Harper finally turned and looked at him. "Yelling at her isn't gonna change that."

"I know," he snapped, then sighed. "I know."

She softened her tone. "You think she planned to tell us like this?"

"No," he admitted. "But I think, once again, that she thought she could handle a problem on her own."

Mrs. Harper crossed her arms. "That girl has always tried to carry the world by herself."

He stared at the kitchen table. "What are we supposed to do?"

She hesitated.

Then said the truth.

"Well... there ain't nothing you can do now," she said quietly. "You saw her."

He looked up.

"Terry's gonna have that baby," Mrs. Harper continued. "By at least December or January."

Neither of them noticed that Lena had been walking down the back steps in the kitchen.

Lena stood frozen, hand on one railing.

A baby? My brother is having a baby?

Her heart thudded loudly in her chest.

"Terry's having a baby?" She asked as they looked over at her, surprised that she was in the room.

Lena didn't hear or say anything else.

She passed out.

TWENTY

THEY DIDN'T SIT in a circle or lined up on the couch.

Jason leaned against the counter.

Bernard stood near the window, arms crossed.

Guang stood at the breakfast bar, elbows planted, staring at nothing.

Terry was the only one seated.

And Terry was still a woman.

"So," Bernard finally said. "We need to talk about the part nobody wants to say out loud."

Terry looked up. "Say it then."

Guang spoke first. "You're gonna have to deliver a baby."

The words landed heavy.

Terry scoffed lightly. "I know what pregnancy dictates."

"That's not what he means," Jason said.

Bernard sighed. "Ter... this isn't just morning sickness and doctor visits anymore. This is labor. Hospitals. Recovery. A whole human being."

Terry shook her head in the negative. "You're all acting like this is permanent."

Jason stepped closer. "Because right now? It looks like it is."

She stood up abruptly. "No. It looks like it because you're assuming the rules still apply."

"The rules always apply," Bernard said gently.

"Not to me," Terry shot back. "Not to *this*."

Guang frowned. "You've been saying that for months."

"And I'll keep saying it," she replied. "Because I can feel it. Whatever did this to me, whatever took away my manhood and emasculated me and made me into this...it's going to undo itself. Soon."

Jason studied her face. "What if it doesn't?"

Silence.

Terry's voice dropped. "It will."

Bernard softened. "And if it doesn't? It's been over six months."

She swallowed. "Then I'll deal with it just like I have been doing."

Guang leaned back. "You're talking like this is something that's happening *to* you, but you're carrying another life now? What happens when you change back, does that just go away, will you be the world's first pregnant man?"

Terry pressed a hand to her stomach without thinking.

"I'm not keeping this body," she said. "I'm not building a future around something that was never supposed to happen."

Jason exhaled slowly. "Okay. But just in case..."

"No," she snapped. "No 'just in case.'"

Bernard raised his hands. "We're not trying to force you accept a life you don't want."

"Then stop talking like I'm already living it."

No one answered that.

Finally, Jason nodded once. "Alright."

He looked at the others. "We move at Terry's pace."

Bernard hesitated, then agreed. "For now."

Terry let out a breath she hadn't realized she was holding.

"Thank you," she said.

***

Christmas came early and quickly that year.

Light fluffy snow continued to fall as it dusted the sidewalks and the parking lot just outside of Terry's apartment building, soft but stubborn.

Inside of her apartment, *Let It Snow'*, by Boys II Men played softly.

A small artificial tree stood in the corner of her living room, undecorated except for white lights.

She stood in front of the mirror, pulling a red sweater down over her stomach.

Eight months.

There was no denying it anymore.

Her hands rested there longer now.

Not in acceptance.

In disbelief.

The world outside was quiet. Too quiet.

One month away.

She stared at her reflection.

"This isn't forever," she whispered.

The lights blinked softly behind her.

She no longer knew if she were trying to convince the universe of her certainty that her

114

situation would change or if she were trying to
convince herself while the universe was telling
her that things were not going back to the way
they used to be.

115

TWENTY-ONE

THE JEEP HUMMED steadily beneath them, tires rolling over quiet suburban asphalt, roads damp from wet snow which had been falling earlier.

Jason drove.

Terry stared out the passenger-side window, her arms were folded tightly across her chest, although one hand remained unconsciously curved around her stomach.

The faint glow of the streetlights slid across her face in passing streaks of amber.

Neither one of them had spoken for several minutes.

Finally, Jason cleared his throat as he checked the rearview mirror.

"You okay?" he asked.

She didn't look at him. "Define okay."

He gave a small exhale. "You're quiet."

"I'm thinking."

"That's usually when I get nervous," he said lightly.

She didn't smile.

The Jeep turned right onto her parents' street. Christmas lights of all kinds clung stubbornly to a few houses, bright and blinking, defiant against the cold.

Jason looked over and tried again. "Your mom said they're hoping to be back from Paris before..."

"Before I go into labor," Terry finished flatly.

He nodded. "Yeah."

Silence again.

He then hesitated. "Have you... thought about names?"

That did it.

Her jaw tightened. Her eyes glistened almost instantly.

"Jason."

"I'm just asking."

"I know you're just asking."

He softened. "I didn't mean anything by it."

She finally turned to him. "You keep talking like this is happening. Like this is real."

He gestured to her stomach. "It is real, Ter."

Her breath hitched. She looked away quickly, blinking hard.

"No," she whispered. "It's not supposed to be."

The Jeep slowed to a stop at a red light.

Jason watched her carefully. "You're eight months pregnant."

"That doesn't make it permanent."

"Terry..."

She shook her head sharply. "Stop trying to romanticize this."

"I'm not."

She nodded her head. "Yes, you are." Her voice trembled now. "You and I were boys and now you're doing the whole hopeful father thing. Talking about names. Talking about delivery dates. Acting like we're going to be a family. Like this whole thing is some... miracle."

"It kind of is."

Her head snapped toward him.

"Don't," she said quietly.

"I'm just saying..."

"Stop." Her voice cracked. "Stop trying to make this into something beautiful. I want my body back, to be the man I was, not...this."

He swallowed.

Terry wiped at her eyes, frustrated with herself and her whole situation.

"If I name it... if I start picking out names... that means I'm accepting it."

"And?"

"And I cannot accept something that isn't supposed to happen from a body I'm not even supposed to have."

She writhed in her seat.

"I am not supposed to be a woman, and I am definitely not supposed to have a baby, period!"

The light turned green. Jason eased forward.

"You don't think it's real," he said carefully. You've been this way for almost eleven months, maybe it's some sort of weird course correction thing."

"Like I was always supposed to have been a female?"

"What other explanation is there for this?"

"I think that something happened or that something is still happening to me," she replied.

"Something that is supernatural and unnatural
at the same time. Something that's still going to
correct itself."

"And if it doesn't?"

She didn't answer.

Then. "It will," she started, "If I was
supposed to always have been a woman and this
was some sort of divine course correction, I
wouldn't have remembered being male! None of
you all wouldn't remember me being male, for
heaven's sake, I have to bribe Lena to keep her
from saying anything to our parents because
she even remembers me as a male, so in my
mind, because of all of that, this...is not meant
to be."

She pressed both hands over her stomach,
as if holding something back.

"I'm not attaching myself to this," she said.
"I'm not building fantasies. I'm not picking
names. That's why despite my parents' wishes, I
didn't have a baby shower!"

Jason's voice softened. "You don't have to
pick one tonight."

"Then stop asking because I don't ever plan
to pick one."

He nodded slowly. "Okay."

He shook his head in the affirmative
realizing that he pushed his best friend too far.
"Okay," he repeated.

They drove the rest of the way in silence.

But Jason's hand hovered briefly over the
gearshift between them, close enough to reach
for hers.

But instead of grabbing it he clenched his hand into a fist.

TWENTY-TWO

DINNER FELT STRANGELY normal.

Too normal.

The dining table was set properly, her mother always insisted on that, cloth napkins, real plates, candles even though it was just the five of them.

The aroma of baked macaroni and cheese, collard greens, candied yams, and an oven roasted chicken dominated the house over the other dishes prepared by Mrs. Harper.

Her father carved the chicken with deliberate precision.

Her mother refilled glasses before anyone asked.

They were trying.

Jason answered questions politely. Where he was working now. How his parents were doing. He didn't mention the conversation had in the jeep a few short moments ago.

Terry felt like she was watching herself from outside her body.

Her mother finally placed her fork down onto her plate. "We'll be gone three weeks," she said gently. "Paris isn't optional."

Her father nodded. "Your mother's conference was booked a year ago."

"But we'll be back before the new year," her mother added quickly. "Plenty of time."

"Plenty of time for what?" Terry asked quietly.

"For your delivery," her mother said.

The word landed softly but firmly.

Jason shifted slightly in his chair.

Her father cleared his throat. "We'll support you, whatever you need."

Terry stared at her plate.

Lena had been unusually quiet the entire meal.

Too quiet.

Finally, Lena spoke.

"So... this is really happening?"

Everyone just looked at her, no one answered immediately.

Her mother gave a careful nod. "Yes."

Lena's eyes moved slowly to Terry's stomach.

"And Jason's the dad?" she asked.

Jason answered gently. "Yeah."

Lena's expression twisted as she looked at everyone, not angry, not confused.

Panicked.

"This just doesn't make sense," she finally cried out.

Terry's head lifted slightly. "Lena..."

"No," Lena said, standing abruptly. Her chair scraped loudly against the floor. "This doesn't make sense."

Lena pointed at Terry's stomach.

"That doesn't make sense!"

"Sit down," her father warned.

But Lena's voice rose.

"She can't have this baby!"

The room froze.

Her mother stood. "Lena..."

"She can't!" Lena shouted, tears springing into her eyes. "She's supposed to be my big brother!"

Silence detonated across the table.

Terry went very still.

Jason's body tensed instantly beside her.

Her father looked like someone had struck him.

Lena's voice broke through the brief silence.

"This...this isn't right. This...isn't how things are supposed to be. I thought you would be a man again by now," she said looking at Terry. "The way this is going on, this isn't normal."

Her mother got up and moved toward her carefully.

"Honey..."

"No!" Lena backed away. "You all keep talking about delivery dates and Paris and support like this is fine!"

Her gaze landed back on Terry as she teared.

"You're supposed to be my big brother."

The words hung there.

Heavy.

Unavoidable.

Terry swallowed slowly.

No one in the room knew how to respond.

TWENTY-THREE

NO ONE MOVED for a long time after Lena's outburst.

The room felt smaller now. Tight. Pressurized.

Terry stood slowly from her chair.

"I need to explain something," she said.

Her father let out a short, humorless breath. "You don't need to explain nothing, it's been eight months...we learned late that you're pregnant, we're all dealing with it in our own way."

"That's not what I mean."

Her mother folded her arms, bracing. "Then what do you mean?"

Terry looked at Jason briefly. He gave a small nod.

She swallowed.

"I wasn't born like this."

Her father's eyebrows pulled together. "Like what?"

"Female."

Silence.

Her mother blinked. Once. Slowly.

"You've always been female," Mrs. Harper said evenly.

"No," Terry replied. "I wasn't."

Her father's jaw tightened. "Terry."

"I was born a male," she blurted. "For twenty-three years I have been your son. Something happened earlier this year. I don't know how. I don't know why. But my body changed."

Her mother stared at her like Terry had just started speaking another language.

"You're saying," her father said carefully, "that you used to be a man."

"Yes."

Jason stood up. "I can vouch for her...him."

Bernard wasn't here; Guang wasn't here, but Jason was.

"I grew up with Terry...we were best friends," he continued. "Before this happened, we were boys."

Lena nodded quickly. "She wasn't like this last year or the year before that or the year before that. I remember."

Her mother shook her head slowly. "You're all talking like this is some kind of science fiction movie."

"It's not," Terry said. "It's my life. I went to sleep one night, a man, and I woke up a woman."

Her father ran a hand over his face. "You expect us to believe that you just...transformed? From a man to a woman?"

"I know how that sounds, but so much happened and when mom saw me and recognized me as a female, I didn't want to stress her out."

"This is nonsense, I remember holding my baby girl for the first time like it was yesterday!"

"I can't explain why my friends remember me as a man or why Lena remembers me as a man, and why you two can't, but I am telling the truth!"

"And the pregnancy?" her mother pressed as she put her fork down hard. "That just happened too?"

"Yes."

Mr. Harper looked at Jason. "You sayin'...that you knew she was a man and you still got her pregnant?"

"No...dad...no, that's not at all what we're saying...that's a whole 'nother story."

Mrs. Harper let out a soft, disbelieving laugh. "So this is what? A miracle? A curse? An accident of biology that nobody else on earth has experienced or documented?"

"I don't know what this is!" Terry's voice cracked. "But it's not normal and it's not permanent, I'm going to change back."

Her father straightened. "You're right about one thing. It's not normal."

Jason stepped in carefully. "Sir, with respect, we wouldn't lie about something like this."

Her father rounded on him. "You wouldn't? Because from where I'm standing, this looks like more than just a lie, it looks like some sort of fantastic or incredible excuse."

"An excuse for what?" Lena asked.

"An excuse that makes everything easier," he snapped. "An excuse where this pregnancy isn't real. Where nobody has to accept it. Where the baby can disappear and nobody gets attached because it was never supposed to be here."

Terry's stomach dropped.

"That's not what this is," she whispered.

Her mother's voice softened, but it cut deeper. "Then what is it? Because from where we are, that's exactly what this looks like."

Terry opened her mouth.

She then closed it.

There were no medical files. No proof. Just memory.

Her father shook his head. "You think we didn't notice? You struggling, you hiding the pregnancy from us? You think we didn't see the denial?"

"I'm not in denial."

"You are," he said firmly. "For months you been acting like this pregnancy, will just go away..."

"Because it will."

Mrs. Harper leaned in closer now, eyes sharp.

"Okay," she said quietly.

The room went still.

"I'll know everything I need to know if you tell me something simple."

Terry's throat tightened.

Her mother looked directly at her.

"What's the baby's name?"

The question hung there.

Simple. Human. Concrete.

Not metaphysical implication in the question. Nothing theoretical. Nothing supernatural.

Just a name.

Jason's eyes shifted toward Terry.

Lena held her breath.

Terry's mind went blank.

She had refused to pick one.

Refused to look at list of names.

She refused to allow herself to imagine.

Her lips parted.

But nothing came out.

Her mother's expression changed first.

Not anger.

Not triumph.

Something worse.

Understanding.

"You don't have one," Mrs. Harper said softly.

Terry blinked rapidly.

"No," she admitted.

Her father exhaled sharply. "Because...like I said, this is your plan."

"It's not a plan!"

"You won't name it," he continued, voice rising now. "Because if you don't name it, you don't attach. If you don't attach, you can give it away. You can pretend this whole thing was a phase."

"That's not fair," Jason said.

"And you!" her father shot back. "You're willing to just let her give your baby up?"

Mrs. Harper's eyes glistened now. "Terry...if... if this baby is a miracle like you're saying...if this was something cosmic and irreversible..."

She hesitated.

"You should be even more inclined to keep it."

The words landed like a verdict.

Terry felt something inside her crack.

Not belief.

Not certainty.

Just the terrifying possibility that her mother might be right about one thing.

No matter how it came to be, if this baby is born, then not only is the baby a miracle, but there is something going on much larger than she could ever imagine.

But, naming it meant surrender.

And she wasn't ready to surrender.

The room sat in silence.

Heavy.

An incomplete conversation which would seemingly remain unresolved.

TWENTY-FOUR

TGI FRIDAYS ON City Avenue was loud in the way chain restaurants always were, forced cheerfulness layered over low conversations and clinking glasses.

The four of them sat in a corner booth.

Terry hadn't touched her food.

Guang stirred his drink absently.

Bernard leaned back with his arms folded.

Jason sat beside Terry, close but not crowding.

"They think I'm lying," Terry muttered.

"They don't think you're lying," Bernard said carefully. "They think you're coping."

"That's worse."

Jason exhaled slowly. "They don't have our context."

"They have twenty-three years of context," Terry shot back. "Twenty-three years of me being their daughter."

"You were," Guang said gently.

She glared at him. "That's not helpful."

He didn't argue.

Bernard leaned forward. "You have to look at this from their perspective; this looks like denial."

"It looks like I'm crazy. Mom...dad, I was a boy even though you saw me as a girl my whole life."

"No," he said. "You're in denial and stressing. That's what they're seeing."

She rubbed her temples. "I told them the truth Mr. psychology major."

"And they don't have a framework for that truth," Jason replied.

Terry looked at him. "You believed me."

"I remember you as a male."

"They didn't." added Guang.

She finally picked up a fry and put it back down.

"They're leaving for Paris," she said quietly. "And the last thing they're going to remember before they get on that plane is thinking I'm delusional."

Jason's expression softened. "So fix that."

She blinked. "How?"

"You don't have to try to convince them of everything regarding your truth," Bernard said softly. "You just have to reassure them you're okay."

Guang nodded. "You don't need them to believe the origin story. You need them to feel peace."

Terry leaned back against the booth.

"I don't want them traveling thinking I'm planning to give this baby away," she admitted.

Jason looked at her carefully. "If things don't change...will you?"

She hesitated.

"No," she said finally.

The word surprised even her.

Bernard caught it.

"Then that's your apology," he said.

She frowned. "For what?"

"For not being clear."

Guang added, "They don't need supernatural explanations. They need reassurance."

Terry stared at the table.

"I don't want there to be animosity," she said quietly. "Not with them, not now."

Jason reached for her hand this time.

She let him take it.

"Then go talk to your mom," he said.

"Why my mom?"

"Because she'll listen first."

Terry swallowed.

For the first time since the dinner with her parents, the frustration inside her shifted.

It wasn't gone.

It was, for the moment, redirected.

TWENTY-FIVE

THE HARPER HOUSEHOLD was quieter than usual. There were no TVs on.

Mrs. Harper stood in the bedroom, folding blouses and placing them into an open suitcase. The bed was covered in neatly stacked clothes. Three passports rested on the nightstand.

Terry lingered in the doorway.

"Your dad and Lena ran out to grab adapters," her mother said without looking up. "Apparently France does not operate on American convenience once you leave the airport."

Terry almost smiled.

"Need help?" she asked.

Mrs. Harper paused.

Then nodded.

"Sure."

Terry stepped towards the bed and picked up a sweater, folding it carefully.

For a few moments, they worked in silence.

Finally, her mother spoke.

"You look tired."

"I am."

"That's normal," Mrs. Harper replied gently. "Eight months of pregnancy is not kind."

Terry exhaled through her nose. "You're not mad?"

"I am worried about you," her mother said. "There's a difference."

Terry's hands stilled.

"I wasn't trying to lie to you."

"I know."

"You don't believe me though."

Mrs. Harper folded a scarf slowly.

"Look at things from our point of view. It's hard for us to believe, but I believe that you believe it," she said honestly.

That stung less than Terry expected.

"I just didn't want you thinking I'm trying to erase this baby," Terry admitted.

Her mother's hands paused.

"Are you?"

Terry shook her head.

"No."

The word came easier this time.

Mrs. Harper studied her face.

"You don't talk about it like someone who's keeping it," she said softly.

Terry looked down at her stomach.

"I was afraid to."

"Afraid of what?"

"That if I let myself accept it... I'd lose myself."

Her mother's expression shifted.

"You don't disappear just because you become a parent," she said gently.

Terry swallowed.

They continued folding in silence.

After a moment, Mrs. Harper smiled faintly. "Have you thought about names?"

Terry inhaled slowly.

This time, she didn't freeze.

"Yes."

Her mother's eyes lifted.

"Well?"

Terry hesitated just long enough for it to matter.

"Ethan."

The word felt strange in her mouth.

Real.

Mrs. Harper's lips parted slightly.

"Ethan," she repeated softly.

Terry nodded.

"I don't know why," she admitted. "It just...feels steady, powerful."

Her mother stepped closer.

"That's a strong name."

Terry's eyes filled, but she didn't look away.

"I don't want you in Paris worrying that I'm going to give him away," she said quietly.

Her mother reached out and cupped her cheek.

"I won't," she replied.

There was no dramatic hug.

No swelling music.

Just two women standing beside a suitcase.

And for the first time, Terry didn't feel alone.

She rested her hand over her stomach.

"Ethan," she whispered again.

And this time, it didn't feel like surrender.

It felt like choice.

TWENTY-SIX

THE PLANE'S CABIN lights were dimmed, the kind of soft blue glow that made time feel suspended.

Mr. Harper slept with his arms folded, head tilted slightly toward the window.

Mrs. Harper slept too, chin dipped toward her chest.

Between them, Lena was curled into the middle seat, mouth slightly open, the exhaustion of the past weeks finally winning her over.

The engines droned like a lullaby.

Mrs. Harper's dream came gently at first.

A kitchen. Sunlight. A little boy sitting at the table, legs swinging, hair uncombed. He was laughing at something—something silly, something small. She could smell pancakes. She could hear her own voice calling him Terry the way mothers call children when they're pretending to be annoyed but aren't.

He looked up at her.

And he was a boy.

Clear as day.

Not a metaphor. Not a feeling. Not a haze.

A boy with her husband's eyes and her own stubborn jaw, cheeks full and bright with youth.

"Mama," he said, like it was the most natural thing in the world.

And in the dream, she didn't question it.

She just loved him.

The scene shifted.

A school hallway. A backpack. A boy's voice cracking as he argued about something unimportant, something that felt like life and death when you were fourteen. Mrs. Harper reached out to smooth his collar.

He pulled away, embarrassed.

She smiled.

A mother's smile.

Then the dream flickered, briefly, like static across a screen.

And for a second she saw Terry as she was now.

Pregnant.

Tired.

An adult.

Her daughter.

Her... something.

The dream couldn't hold the contradiction.

Mrs. Harper jolted awake with a quiet gasp.

She blinked, disoriented.

The cabin lights were still dim. Lena was still asleep between them. The plane's soft chime sounded overhead as a flight attendant's voice murmured something about descent.

Mrs. Harper turned slowly towards her husband.

Strangely enough, he was awake too.

Not fully. But awake enough to be staring forward with a strange, fixed expression, as if he'd come back from somewhere far away.

Their eyes met.

They both looked down at Lena.

Neither spoke.

Lena shifted in her sleep, face pressing deeper into her hoodie.

Mrs. Harper mouthed silently, *Did you...?*

Her husband's eyes narrowed slightly, unsettled.

He gave the smallest nod. *...have a dream about Terry?* he mouthed.

Something passed between them then, not certainty.

But recognition of shared uneasiness.

A shared impossible memory.

Then, a loud beep.

"Ladies and gentlemen, this is your captain speaking...we've begun our initial descent into Paris and expect to be landing at Charles de Gaulle Airport in approximately twenty-five minutes. The current weather in Paris is partly cloudy with a temperature of fifty-two degrees Fahrenheit, or eleven degrees Celsius. Winds are light out of the northwest.

At this time, we ask that you please return to your seats and ensure your seatbelts are securely fastened. Make sure your seat backs and tray tables are in the upright and locked position, carry-on items are properly stowed, and all electronic devices are switched to airplane mode."

Lena stretched and yawned as she switched sides to lean on without ever opening her eyes.

The captain continued. "Local time in Paris is nine forty a. m... on behalf of our entire crew, we'd like to thank you for flying with American Airlines and we hope you've enjoyed the flight. We look forward to welcoming you to Paris shortly. Cabin crew, please prepare the cabin for arrival."

The captain then repeated the same message in French.

Mrs. Harper swallowed hard and glanced down at Lena, still asleep between them. She didn't want to wake her. She didn't want to ruin the fragile calm of the moment.

But she needed to say something.

So she leaned toward her husband, voice barely above the engine hum.

"I dreamt of him," she whispered.

Her husband's throat tightened. His eyes stayed on the seatback in front of him.

"I did too," he murmured.

They didn't say anything else.

They would not say anything when the wheels hit the runway and the plane rolled toward the gate.

They would not say anything until they all three were settled into a country that was supposed to be a distraction, and until Lena was again sound asleep.

***

The hotel room was warm, elegant, and quiet in the way expensive places always were,

140

carpet thick enough to silence footsteps, curtains heavy enough to block the world.

Dinner had been fine. Normal conversation. Forced laughter. Lena had seemed much calmer than she was a few nights back.

They had gotten her to bed without a fight.

Now she slept peacefully in the adjoining room, the door cracked slightly.

Mrs. Harper stood near the window, arms folded, staring out at the Paris lights she couldn't appreciate.

Her husband sat on the edge of the bed, undoing his watch like it weighed too much.

Finally, Mrs. Harper spoke.

"As I started to say earlier, I had a dream."

He looked up instantly.

She turned slowly. "Terry was a boy."

Her husband didn't blink.

His expression went oddly still, like his face was trying not to betray him.

Mrs. Harper frowned. "You too?"

He exhaled once, long and shallow.

"I didn't want to say it on the plane," he admitted.

"You dreamed it too?" she asked.

He swallowed hard. "I dreamed... we had a son."

Mrs. Harper's heart thudded.

"In part of my dream he was..." she struggled for words. "He was little. Maybe eight. He was eating pancakes. He called me mama like it was normal."

Her husband's eyes flicked away, jaw tightening.

"In mine," he said quietly, "I was teaching him to ride a bike."

Mrs. Harper stared at him.

He continued, voice low. "He fell. Scraped his knee. I picked him up and he was mad at me for saying 'shake it off.'"

She let out a shaky laugh that wasn't happy at all.

"And the name?" she asked carefully.

Her husband hesitated.

Then said it.

"Terry."

Mrs. Harper's hand rose to her mouth.

"We... we named him Terry," she whispered.

Her husband looked at her with something close to fear.

"After the dream," he said, "all of these memories came rushing back and I feel ..."

"How is this possible?" she interrupted, voice cracking. "How can we both have the same dream and all these memories suddenly..."

A small sound came from behind them.

A creak.

They both turned.

Lena stood in the doorway in pajamas, hair messy, eyes wide but not sleepy.

She looked at them like she'd been holding this in for weeks.

"I told you," she said simply.

The words hit the room like a stone.

Neither parent spoke.

Lena stepped closer, voice quieter now, almost trembling with vindication.

"He was my brother," she whispered. "And he still is."

Mrs. Harper's eyes filled.

Her husband looked away, face tightening like he was fighting something inside himself.

Lena's expression didn't soften.

She had waited too long for someone to believe her.

"I told you," she repeated.

And this time, neither parent argued.

TWENTY-SEVEN

GREG WAITED UNTIL Jason was alone.

The parking lot was dim, cold air hanging low between cars, the sky the dull gray blue of a Philadelphia evening that couldn't decide if it wanted to rain.

Jason's keys jingled as he walked toward his Jeep.

He didn't see Greg at first.

Not until the shadow peeled away from between two parked cars.

"Yo," Greg called.

Jason stopped.

His body tensed instantly.

"Greg," Jason said, controlled. "What do you want?"

Greg stepped closer, jaw tight, eyes bloodshot with anger.

"You think yawl can just jump me and it's over?" Greg spat to his left. "You and your boy Guang?"

Jason's grip tightened around his keys. "You shouldn't have done what you did to Terry."

Greg laughed once. Sharp. Ugly.

"You think you're some hero now?" he sneered. "You think she's yours?"

Jason's eyes narrowed. "Alright ...back the hell up."

Greg came closer instead.

"I got bruises all over my face," Greg hissed. "I had to lie to my boss. I had to lie to everybody. And you know what?"

Jason didn't move.

Greg's voice dropped.

"I'm not letting that shit go."

Jason set his keys in his pocket slowly.

"Walk away," he said, calm but firm. "Right now."

Greg's nostrils flared. "Or what? You gonna jump me again? You gonna call for your boy?"

Jason's jaw clenched. "I'm not doing this."

He turned toward his Jeep.

Greg lunged.

Jason reacted fast, pivoting, grabbing Greg's arm, trying to shove him back.

But Greg swung hard, fist catching Jason's cheek.

Jason stumbled, regained balance, then drove his shoulder into Greg's chest.

They slammed into the side of the Jeep with a loud metallic thud.

Greg grunted.

Jason grabbed him by the jacket, pushing him back.

"Walk away!" Jason snapped.

Greg's eyes were wild.

He reached into his waistband.

Jason saw the motion and his blood went cold.

"No," Jason breathed.

Greg pulled the gun.

Jason moved without thinking, diving forward, grabbing Greg's wrist, forcing it upward.

They grappled.

The barrel jerked between them.

Greg snarled, trying to wrench free.

Jason's hands strained.

"Greg...don't..."

The gun fired.

A deafening crack.

Both men froze for a fraction of a second from the shock of it.

Then chaos returned immediately.

Jason shoved hard, trying to twist the weapon away.

Greg fought, panicked now, eyes flashing.

They struggled again.

The gun fired a second time.

Another crack.

Louder than the first.

Then Greg's body jerked strangely.

His mouth opened like he wanted to speak.

Nothing came out.

Jason stumbled backward, breath ragged, staring.

The gun slipped from Greg's hand and clattered onto the pavement.

Greg swayed once.

Then collapsed.

Jason looked down at himself and felt heat spreading near his left side.

His knees buckled.

He pressed a hand to his abdomen, blood.

Not a lot, but enough to make the world tilt.

Somewhere nearby, someone screamed.

A car alarm went off.

Jason's vision narrowed.

His legs gave out.

And as the parking lot blurred, the last thing he saw was Greg's body lying unnaturally still beside the Jeep.

TWENTY-EIGHT

THE HOSPITAL SMELLED like antiseptic and pine cleaners and bleach all mixed together. and the lighting was mostly fluorescent.

Terry moved fast, belly heavy, breath sharp with panic as she pushed through the sliding doors.

Bernard stayed close on her left.

Guang on her right.

They were moving as a unit, Jason's name like a drumbeat in Terry's skull.

"Room four-twelve," the nurse had said.

They reached the hallway.

And Terry stopped dead.

Jason lay in the hospital bed.

Handcuffed.

A uniformed officer stood nearby, arms folded.

Jason's face was pale but conscious. His eyes lifted when he saw them.

"Terry, Bernie, G," he said, voice hoarse. "Hey."

They rushed to the bedside, Terry gripping the rail.

"Jason..."

"I'm okay," he said quickly. "It's minor. They said the bullet didn't hit anything vital."

Her hands trembled.

"Why are you handcuffed?" Guang demanded, anger flaring.

The officer glanced at them. "Procedure. Person involved in a shooting."

Jason swallowed. "It was self-defense."

Bernard's eyes narrowed. "What happened?"

Jason exhaled carefully, wincing slightly. "Greg."

The name hit Terry like a slap.

"He literally threw himself at me," Jason continued, voice tight. "He confronted me in the parking lot while I was getting in my car. About him getting beat up. About... everything."

Terry's mouth went dry.

Jason's gaze flicked to her stomach and back to her eyes.

"I tried to get him to walk away, but he persisted. Then he pulled a gun."

Guang cursed under his breath.

Jason kept going. "We fought over it. It went off."

Terry whispered, "Once?"

Jason shook his head no. "Twice."

"One bullet got me, just grazed, they said." He swallowed. "The other..."

He didn't finish.

Bernard's voice lowered. "Greg?"

Jason's eyes shut briefly as he nodded.

"He was hit. He... he didn't make it." Jason's voice cracked slightly. "They pronounced him at the scene."

The room tilted.

Terry felt her blood drain from her face.

Not joy.

Not sadness.

Something worse.

A mixture.

Relief that Jason was alive.

Horror that someone was dead.

Fear of what it meant.

Guilt that she couldn't even name what she felt.

Her knees weakened.

Jason's eyes widened. "Terry..."

"I'm okay," she lied automatically.

Bernard stepped forward. "Terry, sit."

Her vision narrowed.

The last thing she heard was the monitor beeping steadily and Jason saying her name again, urgent and afraid.

Then the world went black.

***

When Terry came to, the lights were softer.

A different room.

A nurse adjusting a cuff on her arm.

Bernard's voice low nearby.

"She's eight months," he was saying. "Are they keeping her for observation?"

"Of course," the nurse replied.

Terry blinked slowly, disoriented.

Her hand moved instinctively to her stomach.

The baby shifted faintly beneath her palm.

Real.

Still real.

Jason was alive.

150

Greg was dead.

Her parents were in Paris looking forward to this baby she didn't want to have.

And she was lying in a hospital bed, caught between lives.

Terry stared at the ceiling.

And for the first time in months, she didn't whisper that it would undo itself.

She just breathed as tears poured out of her eyes.

TWENTY-NINE

TERRY WOKE TO some slight abdominal pressure.

Not pain.

Pressure.

Low and deep.

She didn't move at first. The hospital room was dimmer than before. Late evening now.

The steady hum of machines and distant hallway footsteps blended into background noise.

Her hand was already resting over her stomach.

The pressure came again.

Tighter this time.

Her breath hitched.

Not sharp.

Not stabbing.

But unmistakable.

Her heart rate picked up immediately.

"No," she whispered.

Across the room, Bernard looked up from the chair he had fallen half-asleep in.

"What?"

She swallowed. "Something's... different."

Guang stood quickly.

Jason wasn't there. He was on a different unit altogether, telemetry, she was on the maternity ward.

The pressure rolled through her again.

This time it tightened across her abdomen like a band being slowly pulled.

She gripped the sheets.

Bernard was at her side in seconds.

"Is it pain?"

"I don't know," she said, breath uneven. "It's not sharp. It's just... tightening."

Guang pressed the nurse call button.

Terry's mind raced.

Eight months.

Too early.

Too soon.

The nurse entered quickly, calm but alert. "What are we feeling?"

"Pressure," Terry managed. "Like everything's clenching."

The nurse nodded, already reaching for the monitor.

"Braxton Hicks can be stronger with stress," she said evenly. "Let's take a look."

They adjusted the fetal monitor belt around Terry's abdomen.

The machine began tracing lines across the screen.

The tightening came again.

The line peaked.

Bernard stared at it like it was a bomb countdown.

"Is that bad?" he asked.

The nurse, staring at the monitor, didn't answer immediately. She just watched the rhythm.

Another contraction.

Stronger.

Closer.

Her tone shifted just slightly. "I'm going to call OB."

Terry's pulse pounded in her ears.

Guang's jaw tightened. "Is she going into labor?"

"We're checking," the nurse replied calmly as she left out.

Terry's hands shook.

"This isn't supposed to happen," she whispered.

The words came automatically, the old reflex.

But they sounded different now.

Not denial.

Fear.

A doctor entered within minutes. Efficient. Focused.

"How far apart?" she asked.

"About six minutes."

Terry's eyes widened. "Six?"

The doctor knelt near the bed. "We're going to examine you, okay?"

She nodded, throat tight.

The room moved around her in controlled urgency.

Bernard stood near her shoulder.

Guang hovered near the foot of the bed.

Another contraction.

She inhaled sharply through it.

"Easy," Bernard murmured.

The doctor finished the exam and looked up.

"You're not fully dilated," she said. "But you are contracting consistently."

Terry's vision tunneled slightly.

"What does that mean?" she asked.

"It means," he replied evenly, "we're going to try to stop this."

The word landed.

Stop?

Medication was administered through the IV and the dose adjusted. Instructions were given to the nurse.

"Stress can trigger early labor," the doctor explained. "Your body's been through a shock."

Terry blinked back tears.

Jason.

Greg.

Her parents.

Everything crashing at once.

Another contraction came, but weaker this time.

The doctor watched the monitor carefully.

"Good," she murmured. "It's slowing."

Minutes passed.

Then more.

The peaks on the screen became smaller.

Less frequent.

The tightening faded into residual soreness.

Terry exhaled long and shaky.

"Is he okay?" she whispered.

The nurse smiled gently. "Heartbeat's strong."

The monitor also confirmed it, steady rhythm, unbothered by chaos.

Terry closed her eyes.

Her body felt wrung out.

Exhausted.

But still holding.

The doctor stood. "We're keeping you another night. No debate."

Bernard nodded immediately. "Good."

Guang finally exhaled fully.

Terry stared at the ceiling again.

This time when her hand rested over her stomach, she didn't argue with the reality beneath it.

She didn't tell herself it would undo.

She didn't tell herself it wasn't permanent.

She just whispered softly to herself:

"Relax."

And for now, he did.

THIRTY

THE HOSPITAL ROOM was quieter now. The lights in the hall even seemed to dim down once the night shift came in.

Night had settled fully outside the window. The hallway noise had thinned. Machines hummed softly, no longer urgent, just present.

Terry lay propped up against the pillows, phone pressed to her ear.

Paris was six hours ahead.

Her mother's voice sounded distant, not in tone, but in geography.

"How are you feeling?" Mrs. Harper asked gently.

"Tired," Terry admitted. "But stable. They stopped the contractions."

Her mother exhaled audibly. "Good."

There was a pause.

Not uncomfortable.

Just heavy with things neither of them was saying.

"Your father wanted me to tell you," her mother continued carefully, "that he's proud of how you've been handling yourself."

Terry blinked.

"He is?"

"He won't say it directly to you," Mrs. Harper said softly. "But he is."

Terry swallowed.

"I didn't handle things well at all," she whispered.

"You didn't run," her mother replied. "That counts for a lot."

Silence again.

"Mom?" Terry said quietly.

"Yes."

"I know you don't understand everything."

"I don't," her mother admitted.

"And I know you don't believe all of it."

Another pause.

"No," Mrs. Harper said honestly.

Terry braced herself.

But her mother's voice shifted, warmer now.

"But belief isn't the same as support."

Terry's throat tightened.

"You're my child," Mrs. Harper continued. "Whatever that means. However, that looks. Whatever this becomes."

Terry closed her eyes.

"We may not understand the road," her mother said, "but we will walk it with you."

The words hit somewhere deep.

Not dramatic.

Not explosive.

Just steady.

Terry pressed her hand to her mouth, trying to contain it.

"I don't want you worrying while you're there in Paris," she managed.

"We are always going to worry," her mother said gently. "That's the job."

A faint smile broke through Terry's tears.

"But we are not going to judge," her mother added. "And we are not going to disappear."

Terry couldn't hold it anymore.

The sob escaped quietly.

Not loud.

Not violent.

Just release.

Her shoulders shook as she tried to breathe around it.

On the other end of the line, her mother stayed silent.

Just present.

After a moment, Terry steadied herself.

"I love you," she whispered.

"I know," her mother replied softly. "And we love you."

They said goodnight.

The line disconnected.

Terry wiped her face slowly.

The room felt different now.

Lighter.

Her phone buzzed again.

Bernard.

She answered immediately.

"Tell me something good," she said, voice still fragile.

"I have something better than good," Bernard replied.

Her heart kicked.

"The ballistics report came back."

Terry sat up slightly. "And?"

"Gunshot residue and trajectory matched Greg's angle both times," Bernard said. "The second discharge came from his grip. Jason's prints were only on the slide from trying to redirect it."

Terry's breath stopped.

"So…"

"So he didn't fire the weapon," Bernard finished. "Greg did. Twice."

Her eyes filled again, but this time with relief.

"They're dropping it?" she asked.

"It's clear self-defense," Bernard said. "He'll be exonerated."

The tension she'd been carrying since the hospital doors swung open finally cracked.

A laugh escaped her.

Half sob. Half disbelief.

"Oh my God," she breathed.

"You can exhale," Bernard said gently.

And she did.

A long, full exhale.

She leaned back against the pillows.

"How did you get the information from the report so fast?"

"Girl…how I get my info, I'll never tell."

Terry laughed. "Tell Jason," she whispered.

"I will."

She felt something warm between her legs.

At first, she didn't register it.

Then it continued.

Not contraction.

Not pressure.

Wet.

Her brows furrowed.

"Bernard…" she said slowly.

"Yeah?"

"I think…"

She shifted slightly.

The warmth spread.

Her eyes widened.

"My water just broke."

There was a beat of silence.

Then:

"…What?"

The fluid continued.

Steady.

Real.

Terry stared down at herself, stunned.

The relief hadn't even finished settling before the next wave arrived.

Her voice was calm now.

Almost eerily so.

"Bernard," she said, breath steady. "It's time."

THIRTY-ONE

THE CAMPUS BOOKSTORE was louder than Sorrie expected.

Not loud in the sense of chaos, just alive, it was after all, Christmas break.

Pages were flipping.

Students were selling back textbooks. Some were getting a jump on getting books for next semester.

There were low conversations.

The beep of scanners at the cash registers were spread apart but present.

Someone was laughing too hard near the register.

Life was moving forward in small, ordinary ways.

Sorrie stood near the used textbooks, absently thumbing the corner of a paperback she had no intention of buying as she was looking for a different title.

She wasn't really there.

Her thoughts were elsewhere, unsettled, drifting, tugged by a persistent, uncomfortable feeling she hadn't been able to shake for days.

That was when she heard about her.

"...it's so messed up," a voice said nearby. A woman's voice. Tired. Low. "I still can't believe it happened like that."

Sorrie stilled.

Another voice answered. "He said she's at Temple University Hospital. Like...right now and about to deliver."

A pause.

"And the worst part?" the first voice continued. "I heard it was from a sexual assault. One of her so-called friends."

"That's why I don't have a lot of guys hangin' 'round me like that, chile anything can happen."

"Well my man Bernie is one of her friends but I don't have ta worry about that with him."

Sorrie's grip tightened on the book.

"...what was her name?" someone asked.

There was a brief hesitation, the kind that always came before bad news.

"Terry, Terry Harper," said Lamar.

The world seemed to tilt.

Sorrie turned slowly, careful not to draw attention to herself, her heart suddenly pounding far too hard for her chest.

The three students stood a few feet away, leaning against a display rack, speaking in hushed tones now.

"She used to be, you know," one of them said. "Really confident. Loud. Popular."

"Yeah," the other replied. "People said she changed. Like...really changed."

Sorrie didn't wait to hear any more.

She already knew.

A cold, sinking clarity washed over her, not the sharp thrill of power, not the satisfaction she'd expected when she first cast the spell.

This was something else.

This was weight.

She set the book down and walked out of the store, her pace quickening with every step until she was nearly running.

***

The hospital smelled like antiseptic and urgency.

Phones rang. Shoes squeaked against polished floors. Voices echoed down corridors in clipped, professional tones.

Sorrie moved through it all like a ghost.

She didn't remember getting directions. She didn't remember asking questions. Somehow, she was simply there, outside the maternity wing, her breath shallow, her palms damp.

She could feel it now.

The spell.

Not as a triumph, but as a strain. Stretched thin. Pulled far beyond what she'd intended.

This was never supposed to go this far.

She stepped into the hallway just as a nurse exited a room, gently closing the door behind her.

Through the small window in the door, Sorrie saw movement.

A hospital bed.

White sheets.

A figure sitting upright, shoulders shaking.

Sorrie pushed the door open.

Terry was holding the baby.

Small. Wrapped in pale blue. Breathing softly, unaware of the storm which had brought it into the world.

Terry's face was streaked with tears.

Not loud sobs. Not hysteria.

Just quiet, broken crying, the kind that comes when something inside finally gives way.

"I didn't know," Terry whispered, rocking slightly. "I didn't know love could hurt this much."

Sorrie stopped just inside the room.

Her breath caught.

This wasn't the lesson she'd imagined.

This wasn't humiliation or fear or even understanding earned through discomfort.

This was love.

Complicated. Painful. Unwanted, maybe, but real.

Terry looked down at the child, her voice trembling. "I kept hoping I'd wake up," she said softly. "I kept thinking...maybe tomorrow. Maybe it would all go back."

The baby shifted, tiny fingers curling instinctively.

Terry broke.

Sorrie felt something tear inside her chest.

This wasn't justice.

This was consequence.

She stepped forward, her voice barely more than a breath. "Terry..."

Terry looked up.

Their eyes met.

Recognition flickered, confusion, pain, something older and deeper than anger.

And in that moment, Sorrie knew.

She was too late.

The lesson had already been learned; at a cost she had never meant to demand.

Sorrie's knees weakened.

"I didn't mean for this," she whispered, tears spilling freely now. "I didn't know..."

Terry said nothing.

She only clutched the baby closer, her entire body trembling.

Sorrie reached out, and the room went dark.

The darkness didn't fall all at once.

It pressed in, slowly, like the closing of heavy curtains. The hum of hospital machines dulled. The antiseptic sting in the air faded.

Even Terry's quiet breathing seemed to stretch, thin and distant, as if Sorrie were sinking beneath deep water.

She felt herself unravel.

Not her body, her certainty.

The spell had never been a single act. It was a chain. A ripple she had set in motion without understanding how far it could travel, how many lives it could touch before it finally came to rest.

This isn't how it was supposed to end.

That thought echoed uselessly in the dark.

When sensation returned, it came in fragments.

Cold tile beneath her cheek. The metallic taste of blood where she'd bitten her lip. The muffled sound of voices, urgent, alarmed.

"Miss? Can you hear me?"

Hands helped her sit up. A nurse.

Another voice calling for a doctor. Someone asking if she was family.

She didn't answer.

She couldn't.

Because somewhere beyond the flurry of motion, beyond the well-meaning concern, she felt it, the spell was loosening.

Not snapping. Not exploding.

Unraveling.

Like a knot being patiently undone.

Images rushed through her mind, moments she hadn't witnessed but somehow *knew*.

Terry alone in the dark, sobbing until there was nothing left. The unbearable weight of carrying a body that no longer felt like home. The fear. The shame. The exhaustion.

And beneath it all, a truth Sorrie had never considered:

The magic had not created suffering. It had revealed it.

The spell had forced Terry to live inside the consequences of violence, not as punishment, but as exposure. To vulnerability. To fear. To love twisted by trauma.

It was never justice.

It was transformation without consent.

And that, Sorrie realized too late, was its own kind of cruelty.

She pushed herself upright.

"I need... to see her," she said hoarsely.

The nurse hesitated. "She's resting now."

"Please."

Something in Sorrie's voice, raw, stripped bare, made the nurse nod.

The room was quiet again when Sorrie stepped back inside.

Terry was asleep, the baby nestled against her chest, impossibly small, impossibly real.

Sorrie stood there a long time.

Then, carefully, she whispered "Terry go home!"

Not with anger. Not with righteousness.

But with regret.

The magic slipped away like breath leaving a body.

And Sorrie knew, truly knew, that when Terry woke, the world would be different.

For both of them.

Sorrie turned and left before dawn.

THIRTY-TWO

THE RADIO BLARED as the digital alarm clock flipped to six thirty a.m.

Sleepily, Terry Harper looked at the time as she threw the blanket from overhead and slowly inched her way off the bed.

Aretha Franklin's *Respect* filled the room.

♪What you want... ooh♪♪Baby I got it... ooh♪

Terry shuffled toward the bathroom, every movement heavy, familiar in a way that still surprised her.

She lifted the toilet lid and then stopped and slowly looked towards the mirror.

His face had returned.

Not the softer contours. He looked down and. noticed no swollen belly. No presence of the aching body which had carried weight it was never meant to bear.

Just... him.

Terry touched his cheek.

No shock came. No relief either.

Only something quieter.

Understanding.

He reached into the shower and turned the water on, checking it a few times for temperature.

He then stepped into the shower, letting the heat from the water, then slip over his shoulders. Steam curled around him, blurring the edges of the world.

And there, alone, he cried.

Not because he was a man again.

But because he remembered.

Everything.

The fear. The pain. The helplessness.

He remembered what it felt like to be *changed* without choice.

And for the first time, he understood something he never had before.

He stepped out of the shower, wrapped a towel around his waist, and sat on the edge of the bed.

The song faded and he reached over and turned the radio off.

Silence settled.

Terry looked at the empty room and spoke softly, though he didn't know if anyone was listening.

"I understand," he said.

And somewhere across the city, Sorrie felt the weight lift, not forgiveness, not absolution, but something harder and truer.

Responsibility.

The story didn't end with justice.

It ended with memory and neither of them will ever forget.

****

Later that day, the air felt different.

Lighter.

Sharper.

Honest.

Terry stood outside Anna Homestead's apartment building hands shoved deep into his jacket pockets.

He was himself again.

Fully.

The mirror no longer confused him.

The weight he'd carried for almost a year felt like memory now, not burden.

The door opened before he knocked twice.

Anna stood there, cautious at first.

Then recognition flickered.

"Terry," she said quietly.

He nodded.

They stood there for a moment, measuring the space between past and present.

"I didn't come to disrupt anything," he said gently. "I just... needed to talk."

Anna stepped aside.

He entered slowly.

The apartment smelled faintly of baby powder and laundry detergent.

Small signs of life were everywhere.

He noticed them immediately.

He swallowed.

"I don't know what role I'm supposed to play," he admitted. "I don't know what the rules are."

Anna folded her arms, listening.

"But I know this," he continued. "No matter what has happened to me... no matter what I am going through... that child exists."

He paused.

"And I want to be part of his life."

Anna studied his face carefully.

"You're not confused?" she asked softly.

"No," he said.

For the first time in a long time, he wasn't.

"I'm not here to take," he added. "Or rewrite anything, or change anything you might have going on. I just... want to show up."

Anna's expression softened.

She stepped closer.

"You can," she said.

The words were simple.

But they carried everything.

From down the hallway, a soft cry echoed.

Terry's heart skipped.

Anna glanced back toward the sound.

Then back at him.

"You wanna meet him," she said.

Terry nodded slowly.

Not overwhelmed.

Not afraid.

Just ready.

As he followed her down the hallway, he didn't think about undoing.

He didn't think about correction.

He didn't think about cosmic errors.

He thought about responsibility.

And choice.

And love.

The door to the nursery opened.

And Terry stepped forward.

EPILOGUE

IN THE VAST stretches of space, there are moments that do not belong to any planet.

Not to Earth. Not to stars. Not to time as humans think they understand it.

There are places between outcomes.

And in one of those places, a small light drifted.

It was not a star. It was not quite a soul fully formed. It was something that had happened.

"You are awake," said a deep voice.

The light flickered uncertainly.

"I don't know what I am," it answered.

"That is honest," the voice replied. "Honesty is a beginning."

The light pulsed, faint but steady.

"It's dark."

"Yes."

"Why?"

"Because you were born between two realities," the voice said calmly. "And between realities, there is no sky."

The light tried to move, but movement had no direction here.

"Was I meant to be here?" it asked.

A pause.

"Not quite and you were not to be in this form," the voice admitted. "But you are not nothing."

The light flickered brighter for a moment.

"I think I remember something," it said slowly. "Warmth. A heartbeat that wasn't mine."

"You remember love."

The light trembled.

"I remember being held."

"Yes."

Silence stretched between them.

"Where is she?" the light asked.

"Back in the world that corrected itself."

"Corrected?" the light repeated.

"The spell that was unraveled. The timeline which has been restored. The body returned to where it belonged."

Another pause.

"You remained."

The light dimmed slightly.

"So I was a mistake."

"No," the voice said evenly. "You were an outcome."

The light was quiet for a long time.

"I think I have a name," it said finally.

"Say it."

"Ethan."

The darkness did not react. The voice did not hesitate.

"Hello, Ethan."

The name settled into him like gravity.

"If I go back," Ethan asked, "will she know me?"

"Not the way you want."
Ethan flickered.
"Did she love me?"
"Yes."
The answer came without delay.
Ethan brightened at that.
"I don't want to hurt her," he said.
The voice shifted, almost approving.
"That is wise."
"I don't want to be revenge," Ethan continued. "I don't want to be punishment."
"Good," the voice said solemnly. "Because punishment is simple. Purpose is not."
"What is my purpose?"
"That," the voice replied, "is something you must choose."
A window opened in the darkness.
Not glass. Not a portal. Just clarity.
A small first floor apartment. A nursery. A man standing in a doorway, nervous but steady. A woman holding a child and allowing someone back into the room.
Life continuing.
Ethan watched.
"Who is that?" asked Ethan.
"The man was your mother in the other timeline...the baby is your brother so to speak."
"I was real," he said quietly. "And now..."
"You are still real."
"I am?"
"Yes, just removed and he still has you in his heart."
"I was loved."
"Yes."

The light steadied.

"Then I will not turn that into anger."

The darkness did not close. It expanded.

"Then you are already more than a mistake," the voice said.

Ethan drifted forward.

Not toward Earth. Not yet.

Toward understanding.

And somewhere across a sleeping city, Sorrie felt something settle.

Not forgiveness. Not absolution.

Responsibility.

The story did not end with justice.

It ended with memory.

And the quiet possibility that even unintended creation could choose what it becomes next.

About the Author

Derrick J. Truesdale is a healthcare professional who spent over thirty years wanting to tell the stories he believed would both entertain and inspire. Today, those long-held ideas have become interconnected science fiction and fantasy novels that stand alone while forming a larger, evolving universe.

His worlds can be dark at times—but they are never without purpose. He writes with the hope of encouraging others to explore their imagination, embrace transformation, and discover strength in unexpected places.

Welcome to the world of Semaj, where seemingly separate stories share deeper connections waiting to be discovered

www.SemajBooks.com